The Fourth Plague by Edgar Wallace

Richard Horatio Edgar Wallace was born on the 1st April 1875 in Greenwich, London. Leaving school at 12 because of truancy, by the age of fifteen he had experience; selling newspapers, as a worker in a rubber factory, as a shoe shop assistant, as a milk delivery boy and as a ship's cook.

By 1894 he was engaged but broke it off to join the Infantry being posted to South Africa. He also changed his name to Edgar Wallace which he took from Lew Wallace, the author of *Ben-Hur*.

In Cape Town in 1898 he met Rudyard Kipling and was inspired to begin writing. His first collection of ballads, *The Mission that Failed!* was enough of a success that in 1899 he paid his way out of the armed forces in order to turn to writing full time.

By 1904 he had completed his first thriller, *The Four Just Men*. Since nobody would publish it he resorted to setting up his own publishing company which he called Tallis Press.

In 1911 his Congolese stories were published in a collection called *Sanders of the River*, which became a bestseller. He also started his own racing papers, *Bibury's* and *R. E. Walton's Weekly*, eventually buying his own racehorses and losing thousands gambling. A life of exceptionally high income was also mirrored with exceptionally large spending and debts.

Wallace now began to take his career as a fiction writer more seriously, signing with Hodder and Stoughton in 1921. He was marketed as the 'King of Thrillers' and they gave him the trademark image of a trilby, a cigarette holder and a yellow Rolls Royce. He was truly prolific, capable not only of producing a 70,000 word novel in three days but of doing three novels in a row in such a manner. It was in, estimating that by 1928 one in four books being read was written by Wallace, for alongside his famous thrillers he wrote variously in other genres, including science fiction, non-fiction accounts of WWI which amounted to ten volumes and screen plays. Eventually he would reach the remarkable total of 170 novels, 18 stage plays and 957 short stories.

Wallace became chairman of the Press Club which to this day holds an annual Edgar Wallace Award, rewarding 'excellence in writing'.

Diagnosed with diabetes his health deteriorated and he soon entered a coma and died of his condition and double pneumonia on the 7th of February 1932 in North Maple Drive, Beverly Hills. He was buried near his home in England at Chalklands, Bourne End, in Buckinghamshire.

Index Of Contents

PROLOGUE

South of Florence by some sixty miles, and west of Rome by almost thrice the distance, upon three hills, is Siena, the most equable of the cities of Tuscany.

On the Terzo di Città in I know not what contrada, is the Palazzo Festini.

It stands aloof in its gloomy and dilapidated magnificence, and since it dates from the adjacent Baptistery of S. Giovanni, it leaves the impression of being a crumbling and disgruntled fragment of the sacred edifice that has wandered away in sullen rage to decay at its leisure.

Here, in penurious grandeur, dwelt the Festinis, who claimed descent from none other than Guido Novello, of whom Compagni, the arch-apologist, wrote: "Il conte Guido non aspettò il fine, ma senza dare colpo di spada si parti."*

[* Count Guido did not wait for the end, but departed without a stroke of his sword.]

The Festini was a family to the name of which the Italian nobility listened with immobile faces. And if you chose to praise them they would politely agree; or if you condemned them they would listen in silence; but if you questioned them as to their standing in the hierarchy, you might be sure that, from Rome to Milan, your inquiry would be met by an immediate, but even, change of subject.

The Festinis, whatever might be their relationship with Guido the Coward, effectively carried on the methods of the Polomei, the Salvani, the Ponzi, the Piccolomini, and the Forteguerri.

The vendettas of the middle ages were revived and sustained by these products of nineteenth century civilization, and old Salvani Festini had, as was notoriously evident, gone outside the circumscribed range of his own family grievances, and had allied himself, either actively or sympathetically, with every secret society that menaced the good government of Italy.

It was a hot June afternoon, in the year '99, when a man and two youths sat at their midday meal in the gloomy dining-room of the Palazzo.

The man who sat at the head of the table was, despite his age, a broad-shouldered man of apparent vitality; a leonine head surmounted by a mane of grey hair would have distinguished him without the full beard which fell over his black velvet waistcoat.

Yet, for all his patriarchal appearance, there was something in the seamed white face, in the cold eyes which stared from under his busy brows, which was sinister and menacing.

He ate in silence, scarcely troubling to answer the questions which were put to him.

The boy on his right was a beautiful lad of seventeen; he had the ivory complexion, the perfect, clean-cut, patrician features which characterized the Italian nobility. His lustrous brown eyes, his delicate mouth, his almost effeminate chin, testified for the race from which he sprang.

The young man sitting opposite was four years older. He was at the stage when youth was merging into manhood, with disastrous consequences to facial contours. He seemed thin, almost hollow-jawed, and only the steady quality of his grave eyes saved him from positive ugliness.

"But, father," asked the younger lad, "what makes you think that the Government suspects that you know about the 'Red Hand'?"

The older youth said nothing, but his inquiring eyes were fixed upon his father.

Salvani Festini brought his mind back to the present with a start.

"Eh?" he asked.

His voice was gruff, but not unkindly, as he addressed the boy; and the light of unconscious pride which shone in his eyes as he looked at the youth, softened the forbidding expression of his face.

"I am very well informed, my son," he said with a gentle growl. "You know we have excellent information. The carbineers are pursuing their investigations, and that infernal friend of yours", he turned to the elder son, "is at the head of the inquisitors."

The youth addressed smiled.

"Who is this?" he asked innocently.

The old man shot a glance of suspicion at his son.

"Tillizini," he said shortly. "The old fool, why doesn't he keep to his books and his lectures?"

"He has been very kind to me," said the younger man. He spoke thoughtfully, reflectively. "I am sorry he has annoyed you, father; but it is his business, this investigation of crime."

"Crime!" roared the old man. "How dare you, a son of mine, sitting at my own table, refer to the actions of the 'Red Hand' as crime!"

His face went red with rage, and he cast a glance of malevolence at his heir which might well have shocked a more susceptible man.

But Antonio Festini was used to such exhibitions. He was neither embarrassed nor distressed by this fresh exhibition of his father's dislike. He knew, and did not resent, the favouritism shown to Simone, his brother. It did not make him love his brother less, nor dislike his father more.

Antonio Festini had many qualities which his countrymen do not usually possess. This phlegmatic, philosophical attitude of mind had been bred in him. Some remote ancestor, cool, daring, possibly with a touch of colder blood in his ancestry, had transmitted to this calm youth some of the power of detachment.

He knew his father hated the old professor of anthropology at Florence; for the Festinis, even to this day, preserved the spirit of antagonism which the Sienese of half a thousand years ago had adopted to the Florentine.

There were schools enough in Siena; a college most famous for its lawyers and its doctors.

Simone was graduating there, and what was good enough for Simone should surely be good enough for Antonio.

But the elder son had chosen Florence with that deliberation which had always been his peculiarity, even from his earliest childhood, and in face of all opposition, in defiance of all the Festini tradition, it was to Florence he went.

Tillizini, that remarkable scientist, had conceived a friendship for the boy; had taken him under his wing, and had trained him in his own weird, irregular, and inconsequent way.

Tillizini was a master of crime, and he possessed an encyclopaedic knowledge of men. He was at the beck and call of the secret police from one end of Italy to the other, and, so rumour said, was in receipt of retaining fees from the governments of other nations.

It was Tillizini who had set himself to work to track down the "Red Hand" which had terrorized the South of Italy for so many years, and had now extended its sphere of operations to the north.

And it was a hateful fact that his work had been crowned with success. His investigations had laid by the heels no less a person than the considerable Matteo degli Orsoni, the Roman lawyer, who, for so many years, had directed the operations of one of the most powerful sections of the "Red Hand."

There was something like fear in the old man's breast, though he was too good a Festini to display it; and it was fear which leavened his rage.

"You shall hear a different tale of this Tillizini," he growled, "mark you that, Antonio. Some day he will be found dead, a knife in his heart, or his throat cut, or a bullet wound in his head, who knows? The 'Red Hand' is no amusing organization." He looked long and keenly at his son. Simone leant over, his elbows on the table, his chin resting on his hands, and eyed his brother with dispassionate interest.

"What does Tillizini know of me?" asked the old man suddenly. "What have you told him?"

Antonio smiled.

"That is an absurd question, father," he said; "you do not imagine that I should speak to Signor Tillizini of you?"

"Why not?" said the other gruffly. "Oh! I know your breed. There is something of your mother in you. Those Bonnichi would sell their wives for a hundred lira!"

Not even the reference to his mother aroused the young man to anger. He sat with his hands thrust into the pockets of his riding breeches, his head bent a little forward, looking at his father steadily, speculatively, curiously.

For a few minutes they stared at one another, and the boy on the other side of the table glanced from father to brother, from brother to father, eagerly.

At last the old man withdrew his eyes with a shrug, and Antonio leant across the table, and plucked two grapes from a big silver dish in the centre, with a hand to which neither annoyance nor fear contributed a tremor.

The old man turned to his favourite.

"You may expect the birri here to-day or to-morrow," he said. "There will be a search for papers. A crowd of dirty Neapolitans will go rummaging through this house. I suppose you would like me to ask your friend, Tillizini, to stay to dinner?" he said, turning to the other with a little sneer.

"As to that, you must please yourself, father; I should be very delighted if you did."

"By faith, you would," snarled the old man. "If I had an assurance that the old dog would choke, I'd invite him. I know your Tillizini," he said gratingly, "Paulo Tillizini." He laughed, but there was no humour in his laughter.

Antonio rose from the table, folded his serviette into a square and placed it neatly between the two Venetian goblets which were in front of him.

"I have your permission to retire?" he said, with a ceremonious little bow.

A jerk of the head was the only answer.

With another little bow to his brother, the young man left the room. He walked through the flagged and gloomy hall to the ponderous door of the Palazzo.

A servant in faded livery opened the door, and he stepped out into the blinding sunlight. The heat struck up at him from the paved street as from a blast furnace.

He had no definite plans for spending the afternoon, but he was anxious to avoid any further conflict with his father; and though he himself did not approve of the association which his house had formed with the many desperate, guilty bands which tyrannized over Italy, yet he was anxious to think out a method by which the inevitable exposure and disgrace might be avoided.

There was no question of sentiment as far as he was concerned. He had reached the point where he had come to regard not only his father, but his younger brother, so eager to assist and so anxious for the day when he would be able to take an active part in the operations of the League, as people outside the range of his affections.

It was natural that he should gravitate towards the Piazza del Campo. All Siena moved naturally to this historic fan-like space, with its herring-boned brick pavement, and its imperishable association with the trials and triumphs of Siena.

He stood by the broad central pavement which marks the course of the Pallio, deep in thought, oblivious of the many curious glances which were thrown in his direction. For despite the heat of the day, all Siena was abroad.

Had he been less engrossed by his thoughts, he might have regarded it as curious that the Sienese, who hold this hour sacred to the siesta, should have so thronged the square and the street, on a hot June afternoon.

Standing there, absorbed by his thoughts, he heard his name spoken softly behind him, and turned.

He snatched off his soft felt hat with a smile, and extended his hand.

"I did not expect to see you, Signor Tillizini," he said.

The pleasure of the meeting, however, was over-clouded a second later, as he realized with a sense of apprehension that the old professor's visit was not without gloomy significance to his house.

Professor Tillizini, at that time, was in his eightieth year. As straight as a die, his emaciated and aesthetic face was relieved by two burning eyes in which the soul of the man throbbed and lived.

He took the arm of his pupil and led him across the piazza at a slow pace.

"Antonio mio," he said with grave affection, "I am come because the Government desires certain information. You know, although I have not told you, that we are inquiring into a certain organization."

He laid his thin white hand upon the other's shoulder, and stopped, peering down into the boy's face with keen attention.

"Antonio," he said slowly, "that investigation is to be directed toward your father and his actions."

The other nodded. "I know," he said simply.

"I am glad you know," said Tillizini, with a little sigh of relief. "It has rather worried me. I wanted to tell you some time ago that such an inquiry was inevitable, but I did not think I would be doing my duty to the State if I gave that information."

Antonio smiled a little sadly.

"It does not matter, Signor," he said; "as a matter of fact, my father knows, and is expecting you."

Tillizini nodded.

"That I expected too," he said, "or rather let me be frank, I hoped he would be; for a policeman expected is a policeman defeated," he smiled.

They walked a little way in silence, then—

"Are you satisfied in your mind that my father is concerned in all these outrages?" asked Antonio.

The old man looked at him sharply.

"Are you not also?" he asked.

The heir of the Festinis made no reply. As if by mutual consent they changed the subject and spoke of other matters.

The old man was awaiting the arrival of the police officers; that much Antonio guessed.

They spoke of the college at Florence and of mutual friends. Then, by easy stages, the professor approached his favourite subject, the subject of his life-work.

"It is a thousand pities, is it not?" he said, "that, having got so far, the good God will not give me another hundred years of life?"

He smiled and shrugged his shoulders.

"At the end of which time I should require another hundred," he said philosophically. "It is as well, perhaps, that we cannot have our desires. "It would have satisfied me," he continued, "had I a son to carry on my work. Here again I am denied. I have not, I admit," he said, with that naiveté which was his charm, "even in my life provided myself with a wife. That was an oversight for which I am now being punished."

He stopped as a tall officer in the uniform of the carbineers came swinging across the Piazza del Campo, and Antonio Festini instinctively stepped away from his master's side.

The two spoke together, and by and by, with a little nod of farewell and a fleeting shadow of pity in his eyes, Tillizini accompanied the tall officer in the direction of the Palazzo Festini.

Antonio watched him until he was out of sight. Then he resumed his aimless pacing up and down the Piazza, his hands behind his back, his head sunk forward on his breast.

Tillizini accompanied the tall officer to the Festini Palace. He pulled the rusty bell that hung by the side of the great door, and was admitted.

He was conducted with all the ceremony which his obvious rank demanded, for was not there an officer of carbineers accompanying him, and did not that officer treat him with great deference? to the big salon of the Festinis.

It was an apartment bleak and bare. The ancient splendours of the painted ceiling were dim and dingy, the marble flagged floor was broken in places, and no attempt had been made to repair it. The few chairs, and the French table which had been pushed against the wall, seemed lost in that wilderness of chilly marble.

In a few moments Count Festini came in. He was still dressed in his velvet coat and waistcoat, and the riding breeches and boots which he and his sons invariably wore, for they were great horsemen, and had but that one taste in common.

He favoured Tillizini with a bow, which the professor returned.

"I am at your Excellency's disposition," he said formally, and waited.

"Count Festini," said Tillizini, "I have come upon an unpleasant mission."

"That is regrettable," said Count Festini shortly.

"It is my duty to ask you to allow me to conduct a personal examination of your papers."

"That is not only unfortunate, but outrageous," said Festini, yet without the sign of irritation which the carbineer officer, his fingers nervously twitching the whistle which would summon his men, had expected.

"It is not my wish," Tillizini went on, "to make this visit any more disagreeable to your Excellency than is necessary, therefore I ask you to regard me rather as a friend who desires to clear your name from aspersions which—"

"You will spare me your speeches," said Count Festini shortly. "I know you, Paulo Tillizini. I thought you were a gentleman, and entrusted you with the education of my son. I find you are a policeman. In these days," he shrugged his shoulders, "the Italian nobility, and if I remember aright, you come from the house of one Buonsignori?"

Tillizini bowed.

"In these days," Festini went on, "it is necessary, I presume, for our decaying nobility to find some means of providing portions for their marriageable daughters."

"In my case," said Tillizini, "that is unnecessary."

He spoke suavely and calmly: every word which Count Festini had uttered was, by the code which both men understood, a deadly insult. Yet Tillizini preserved the same outward show of unconcern which Festini had seen so disastrously reproduced in his son.

"I can only add," the old man went on, "this one fact, that to whatever depths a member of a noble house may sink in assisting the State to bring justice to the men who are setting the laws of the country at defiance, it is possible, Signor, for a man to sink still, lower, and to be one of those whose dreadful acts, and whose cruel practices, set the machinery of the law in motion."

He spoke in his passionless, even tones, and a red flush crept over the Count's face.

"You may search as you wish," he said. "My house is at your disposition. Here are my keys."

He produced from his pocket a steel ring on which a dozen keys hung.

Tillizini made no attempt to take them.

"If you will conduct me to your bedroom," he said, "I shall not trouble you with any further search."

For a second only Count Festini hesitated. A swift cloud of apprehension passed across his face. Then with a bow he extended his hand to the door.

He followed them into the hall and led the way up the stairs. His room was a large one, facing the road. It was as poorly furnished as the remainder of the house. Tillizini closed the door behind him, and the officer stood, barring all egress.

"Here are my keys."

Again Count Festini held out the polished bunch.

"Thank you, I do not want them," said Tillizini. He stood squarely before the man. "I think it is as well, Count," he said gently, "that I should tell you what I know. Four days ago a man was arrested in the act of placing a bomb on the railway line between Rome and Florence. He was apparently a new recruit, but after he was arrested it was discovered that he was a man who stood very high in the councils of the Florentine branch of your excellent society."

Festini said nothing. He listened with every interest.

"In some way," Tillizini went on, "this man had discovered many secrets which I am sure the 'Red Hand' had no intention of revealing. He may have acted as secretary to one of the heads of your Order. At any rate, he knew that documents incriminating yourself and a very large number of influential people in Italy were secreted in this house."

"Indeed!" said Festini, coldly. "You have the keys; you may verify for yourself the truth of your informant's statement." Again Tillizini made no attempt to take the keys from him.

"He knew more than I have told," he said slowly. "He indicated to me a hiding-place which I gather is known only to you and to the leaders of your band."

He walked to the end of the room, where four long windows lit the apartment. Between the second and the third hung a picture in a deep gold frame. He passed his hand gingerly over the scroll-work on the left side of the frame.

Presently he found what he wanted, and pressed.

The bottom half of the rich carving opened like a narrow drawer.

Festini watched him, motionless, as he took a bundle of papers from the secret recess behind the hinge moulding.

Tillizini examined them briefly at the window and placed them carefully in the inside pocket of his coat. He looked at Festini long and earnestly, but before he could speak the door was opened and Simone Festini came in quickly.

He walked to his father.

"What is it?" he asked, and bent his angry brows upon the old professor.

"It is nothing, my son," said Count Festini.

He laid his hand upon the boy's head and smiled.

"You must go downstairs until I have finished my business with his Excellency."

The boy hesitated.

"Why should I go?" he asked.

He scented the danger and was hard to move. He looked round from one to the other, alert, suspicious, almost cat-like.

"If anything should happen to me, Simone," said Count Festini softly, "I beg you to believe that I have provided for you handsomely, and there is a provision which is greater than any I can offer you, the protection and the friendship, and as I hope one day, the leadership, of comrades who will serve you well. And now you must go."

He bent down and kissed the young man on the cheek.

Simone went out, dry-eyed, but full of understanding. In the hall below he came face to face with his brother, who had returned from the Piazza.

"Come this way, Antonio," said the boy gravely.

He walked first into the dining-room where an hour ago they had been seated together at their meal.

"Our father is under arrest, I think," he said, still coolly, as though he were surveying a commonplace happening. "I also think I know what will happen next. Now, I ask you, which way do you go if I take up our father's work?"

His eyes were bright with suppressed excitement; he had grown suddenly to a man in that brief consciousness of impending responsibility.

Antonio looked at him sorrowfully.

"I go the straight way, Simone," he said quietly. "Whichever way is honest and clean and kindly, I go that way."

"Buono!" said the other. "Then we part here unless God sends a miracle, you to your destiny and I to mine."

He stopped and went deadly white, and looking at him, Antonio saw the beads of sweat upon his brow.

"What is the matter?" he asked, and stepped forward to his side, but the boy pushed him back.

"It is nothing," he said, "nothing."

He held himself stiffly erect, his beautiful face raised, his eyes fixed on the discoloured decorations of the ceiling.

For he had heard the pistol shot, muffled as it was by intervening doors and thick walls, that told the end for Count Festini.

Tillizini, hurrying down to break the news to him, found him fully prepared.

"I thank your Excellency," said the boy. "I knew. Your Excellency will not live to see the result of your work, for you are an old man, but if you did, you will behold the revenge which I shall extract from the world for this murder, for I am very young, and, by God's favour, I have many years to live." Tillizini said nothing, but he went back to Florence a sad man.

Three months afterwards he again visited Siena, and in the Via Cavour, in broad daylight, he was shot down by two masked men who made good their escape; and, in his chair, at the College of Anthropology at Florence, there reigned, in good time, Tillizini the younger.

I — SIR RALPH DELIVERS JUDGMENT

It was absurd to call the affair "the Red Hand Trial," because the "Red Hand" had played no part in the case so far as the burglary was concerned.

It was a very commonplace burglary with a well-known, albeit humble member of Burboro's community in the dock. He had been found in a house in the early hours of the morning, he had given an incoherent explanation to the alert butler who had captured him, and, beyond a rigmarole of a story that some mysterious Italian had sent him thither, there was no hint of the workings of the extraordinary association which at the moment agitated the law-abiding people of Britain.

It was equally absurd and grossly unfair to accuse the newspapers who referred to it as "the Red Hand Case," of unjustifiable sensationalism. After all, there was an Italian mentioned in connexion with the charge, quite enough in those days of panic to justify the reference.

The Session House was crowded, for the case had excited more than usual interest. All the county was there. Lady Morte-Mannery occupied a seat on the Bench, as was her right. Most of the house-party from East Mannery had driven over and was seated in privileged places, to the no small inconvenience of the Bar and the representatives of the Press, the latter of whom bitterly and indignantly resented this encroachment upon their already restricted domain.

But Sir Ralph Morte-Mannery, the Chairman of the Session, had a short way with critics and professed, though his practice did not always come into line with his theory, that the Press might be ignored and impressed with a sense of its own unworthiness.

The Pressmen in the Session House at Burboro' were constantly undergoing that mysterious process which is known as "being put in their place." They desired, most earnestly, that the principle should be applied now, for their places were occupied by the guests of the Chairman.

Hilary George, K.C., sat with his colleagues, though only as a spectator. He was curious to see in operation the workings of justice, as Sir Ralph conceived it.

Sir Ralph's sentences were notorious, his judgments had before now come up for revision. He was, perhaps, the best hated man in the country. Mothers frightened their obstreperous children with references to Sir Ralph. He was the bogey man of the poacher, a moral scarecrow to tramps, people who slept out at night, and suchlike dangerous characters.

A little man, spare and bony, his clothes, though carefully fitted, seemed to hang upon him; his face was long and white, and solemn; his lips drooped mournfully at each corner. A pair of gold-mounted pince-nez struck an angle on his pendulous nose as to suggest that they were so placed in order not to obstruct his line of vision. His hair was white and thin; he had two dirty-grey tufts of side-whisker, and affected a Gladstonian collar. His voice, when he spoke, was querulous and complaining; he gave the impression that he felt a personal resentment toward the unfortunate prisoner in the dock, for having dragged him from his comfortable library to this ill-ventilated court.

Sir Ralph was a man hovering about the age of sixty. His wife, who was looking supremely lovely in her black velvet cloak and her big black hat, which one white feather lightened, was nearly thirty years his junior. A beautiful woman by some standards. Junoesque, imperial, commanding; her lips in repose were thin and straight, and if the truth be told, a little repellent. Some people found them so. Hilary George, for one, a daring rider to hounds, and wont to employ the phraseology of the field, confessed that he never saw those lips tighten but a voice within him uttered the warning, "'Ware! 'ware!"

She was a beautiful woman, and a disappointed woman. She had married Sir Ralph Morte-Mannery, five years before, in the supreme faith that she had emerged for ever from that atmosphere of penury which had surrounded her girlhood; that she had said "good-bye" to the strivings, the scrimpings and the make-believe of shabby gentility with which a mother with social aspirations and an income of a £150 a year had enclouded her.

But Vera Forsyth found she had moved from an atmosphere of penury enforced by circumstances to an atmosphere of penury practised for love of it. Sir Ralph was a mean man, he was little short of a miser, and he had the settled conviction that, in taking care of the pennies, he was appointed as by divine right, the natural heir to hundreds.

It seemed to her, in her first year of marriage, that she could never escape from the eternal account book. He was a man who believed in domestic stock-taking. He knew, better than she, the prevalent price of potatoes, and he noted with pain any advance in the grocer's bill, and set himself the congenial task of discovering the cause for any such swollen expenditure.

Now she looked along the Bench at her husband curiously; he was always a source of interest to her. She needed some such interest to sustain her in her everyday acquaintance with this man.

He was summing up with gross partiality. Though he had had one or two bad raps from the Court of Criminal Appeal, he was not to be turned from his set purpose, which was to rid the country of those who showed a disinclination to distinguish the difference between meum and teum.

All who knew the circumstances realized that the summing up was in the veriest bad taste. The young man, white of face, who stood by the dock's edge, his shaking hands clasping and unclasping the iron rail before him, was being tried for burglary, and the burglary was at Sir Ralph's own place.

"He has told you, Gentlemen of the Jury," went on Sir Ralph in his speech, "that a mysterious Italian asked him to break into the house, where somebody would be waiting to give him an equally mysterious packet. He did not intend to steal, so he tells you; he was merely carrying out the instructions of this mythical, perhaps I ought not to say 'mythical,'" said Sir Ralph hastily, with the recollection of a Lord Chief Justice's comments on a judgment of his, "but which may to you, Gentlemen of the Jury, appear to be a mythical person.

"He tells you that he was induced by his poverty to go to Highlawn at midnight, to effect an entrance through the kitchen, and there to wait until some cloaked, masked individual brought him a packet which he was to bring away. He tells you that he had no intention whatever of robbing the owner. He was merely being the accomplice of some person in the house."

Sir Ralph leant back with a little contemptuous smile.

"Well, Gentlemen of the Jury," he said, throwing out his hands, with pseudo good-nature, "if you believe that, of course you still must convict the man on the charge of being an accomplice. As you know, there is in this house a very valuable collection of Renaissance jewellery; and when the Counsel for the Crown tells you, as he has told you, that the inference to be drawn from the man's presence in the kitchen, where the butler discovered him, is that he intended to make a raid upon that jewellery, you are, perhaps, as justified in believing that suggestion as you are in believing that of the prisoner's Counsel, that he was merely acting as an innocent agent in the matter."

He said a few more words, summarized such of the evidence as had not come under his previous purview, and commended the jury to their deliberations with the air of benevolence which invariably enwrapped the peroration of his more malignant speeches.

The jury tramped out, and a buzz of conversation overhung the court. The prisoner lingered a little by the rails; he looked down at the delicate face of his girl-wife, this woman of seventeen, who had sat throughout the trial tense and haggard, listening to the evidence.

"It can't be helped, dear," he said. He was a man of the working classes, but his voice showed an unusual culture.

The girl could only raise her piteous eyes to his; her lips trembled, she could frame no answer. She knew that her young husband spoke the truth. Poverty had ground them down to desperation, but to whatever end it might drive them, it would never make her man a thief.

The jury were back in five minutes. They shuffled into the box, and answered to their names, keeping their eyes averted from the prisoner at the Bar. The Clerk of Assizes put his questions to them.

"Do you find the prisoner 'Guilty' or 'Not Guilty' of the crime of burglary?"

"Guilty," said the foreman, in a high, nervous voice.

Sir Ralph nodded his head approvingly. He turned to the prisoner as the Clerk said, "Have you anything to say before the sentence is passed?"

The man in the dock took a swift glance at the drooping figure of his wife. She had fainted, and a kindly policeman was lifting her to carry her from the court.

"The story I have told," he said, speaking clearly and without hesitation, "was a true story. I had no idea of burgling your house, Sir Ralph. I merely went there because I thought I was acting as the agent of somebody who was carrying on some sort of—" he hesitated. "I hardly like to say it, some sort of intrigue," he continued boldly, "and did not want this fact to leak out."

His eyes roved round the Bench and halted when they met those of Lady Morte-Mannery. They looked at each other; she calmly, incuriously, he hopefully, with a wondering, puzzled stare.

"It is my first offence," he went on. "I have never been in this position before, and although the jury have found me 'Guilty,' my lord, I do hope that you will take a lenient view of my offence, not only for my own sake, but for the sake of my wife and unborn child." His voice shook a little as he pleaded. It was the only sign of emotion he had given.

Sir Ralph nodded again. It was a grim nod. It put a period to the prisoner's speech. The Chairman adjusted his gold pince-nez, and bent his head from left to right, consulting his colleagues.

"Your offence, George Mansingham," he said, "is peculiarly abhorrent to me. I do not consider the fact that the house burgled was my own. Fortunately I am unaffected by personal considerations, and the fact that I, myself, was away from home that night enables me to try this case in an unprejudiced spirit."

He looked down at the paper on his desk musingly. Then he suddenly jerked his head up.

"You will be kept in penal servitude for seven years," he said.

Something like a gasp ran through the court. Hilary George, monocle in eye, half started to his feet, then sank back again. The man in the dock stood dazed.

"Seven years," he repeated, and shook his head as though he could not understand it, then turned and stepped down the stairs which led to the cells below.

Hilary George was a stout man; he had a large fresh face, and eyes that told plainly of his immense vitality and joy of life. Seeing him you thought of an overgrown boy, and the monocle, as a friend had remarked, seemed out of place in one so young. He had one of the biggest practices at the Bar; he was a skilful lawyer and a brilliant debater.

You might think him an easy man to manage, with his parted lips that showed two rows of white even teeth and that look of surprise and delight which shone in his eyes. But no man who had ever tried to persuade Hilary George against his will or against his better judgment, had ever repeated the attempt.

He stood now, an immaculate figure, on the steps of the Session House. He was not smiling, he looked as grave as his facial conformation would allow. Very slowly, very deliberately, he buttoned the white gloves over his huge hands. He looked at his watch, and, as he did so, the East Mannery party came out, Lady Morte-Mannery a little ahead, Sir Ralph following with two or three of his guests.

"Will you drive over in the car with us, or will you take the wagonette," asked Sir Ralph, pleasantly. He was rather in awe of the big barrister, as much in awe as he could be of anybody, and he invariably cloaked his uneasiness with a certain perkiness of manner which passed with Sir Ralph for good-humour.

"I'm not coming over, Ralph," said Hilary George, quietly.

The Chairman raised his brows.

"Not coming over?" he repeated. "What do you mean?"

"I'm going back to town," said Hilary, slowly as before.

"But why? What has happened? I thought you were keen on the shooting."

"I'd rather not say why," said Hilary. "If you'll be good enough to tell my man to bring my boxes to the station, I'll amuse myself in Burboro' for another hour."

"But what is the reason?" persisted Sir Ralph. "Have you had any news? Is there any necessity for your going back to town?"

Hilary scratched his chin reflectively.

"I'll tell you," he said, and faced the other squarely. "You've just sentenced a man to seven years penal servitude."

"Yes?" replied Sir Ralph, wonderingly.

"It was a perfectly beastly sentence," said the K.C., and every word cut like a knife. "A perfectly beastly, malicious, vindictive, unjust sentence," he repeated, "and I would not stay another hour in the house of the man who passed it.

"More than this!" he said, with a sudden accession of fierceness and benevolent malignity, if the paradox may be allowed, which almost paralyzed his hearer, "I will not rest until that sentence is reduced. My solicitors shall take it to the Court of Appeal."

"You, you, how dare you!" spluttered Sir Ralph.

"A perfectly beastly sentence," repeated the other, with annoying deliberation. "Don't talk to me, Sir Ralph, I'm not a tyro, I'm a barrister. I know the game better than you. I know what sentence was justifiable there. I know exactly how your own personal prejudice stepped in to confine this man, this young man, a first offender, to a living hell."

He spoke with vehemence, his plump face growing redder and redder as his anger rose.

"I will never forgive you, Hilary," cried Sir Ralph, shaking with anger. "You have mortally offended me. You know I believe in long sentences."

"I don't care a damn what you believe in,'' said the other, and his very calmness emphasized the strength of his language. "I bid you good morning."

He walked over to where Lady Morte-Mannery stood watching them.

"I am sorry, Lady Morte-Mannery," he said, a little stiffly. "I shall not be coming back to the house. An important engagement has called me to London."

She murmured her sorrow conventionally, though she was by no means displeased to see the back of a man whom at first she had regarded as one who might easily be influenced to her views. Her views, it may here be remarked, were peculiar.

"Why has he gone?" she asked her husband, as the car drove through the main street of Burboro'.

Sir Ralph, who was glowering with rage, vouchsafed a snarling answer.

"How do I know? Why do you ask ridiculous questions? Because he's a fool," he went on viciously. "Because he's a blackguard. He's grossly insulted me, and I'll never forgive him." He was in a white heat of temper, and for the whole day brooded on the affront which had been offered him.

Vera made one or two ineffectual attempts to smooth his ruffled plumage. She was particularly anxious to get him into a good mood. She had one or two requests to make, which in his present frame of mind she knew would be rejected without thought. Her efforts were unavailing.

"I wish you wouldn't potter round," he growled, when she went into the library on the pretext of tidying away some books which had been left out by some careless guest.

"Oh, come here," he said, as she was going out of the room. "Here's a bill from Burt's. How many packets of prepared oats did we have in last week?"

"I forget, dear," she said.

"Six," he growled. "Do you know we have never had more than four before?"

"Mr. George liked it for breakfast," she answered.

"Mr. George!" he almost shouted. "Don't mention that man's name. Why is Bulgered charging 1s. 0½ d. a pound for his beef? It's monstrous, change the butcher. I wish to goodness you'd show some interest in the conduct of your house, Vera."

He scowled at her under his white shaggy brows.

"You go on as if I was made of money. Practise some sense of economy. My dear girl, before you were married you counted every penny. Imagine they are your mother's, and count mine."

With a shrug, she left him. He was utterly impossible in these moods. She went into the drawing-room wondering how she should approach her lord on the subject which lay uppermost in her mind. A girl sat in one of the windows, reading. She looked up with a smile as Vera entered.

"Isn't it a bore?" she said. "They've just told me that Mr. George has gone back to town. He played such beautiful piquet. Why has he gone?"

She rose lazily, putting her book down. She was a tall, beautiful girl, of that exquisite colouring which is the English gentlewoman's heritage. The well-poised head was crowned with a luxurious mass of russet gold hair. Her eyebrows, two delicate lines of jet black, were set over a pair of the loveliest eyes that man ever looked into. At least, so thought many a man who knew her. Even Sir Ralph, self-engrossed and contemptuous, he said, of beauty, had commented upon their liquid loveliness.

A straight nose, and a firm, rebellious chin, a perfectly calm mouth, completed the picture. As she moved she displayed the grace of her slender figure. Every movement suggested the life of freedom, freedom of field and road, eloquently, as did her complexion of the softening qualities of her native Ireland.

"The horrible thing about being a poor relation," she said, as she dropped her strong hand affectionately on the other's shoulder, "is that one can't command the friends of one's rich relations. I should have told Hilary George: 'You cannot go to London, however pressing your business may be, because my niece Marjorie, wants somebody to play piquet with her.'"

Vera shook the hand from her shoulder with a scarcely perceptible movement.

"Don't be silly, Marjorie," she said a little tartly. "Ralph's very worried. Hilary has been awfully rude to your uncle."

The girl's eyebrows rose.

"Rude?" she repeated. "Why, I thought they were such good friends."

"He has been very rude," she said again. "By the way," she said, "your man is coming down to-day, isn't he?"

The girl's face flushed. She drew herself up a little.

"I wish you wouldn't say that sort of thing, Vera," she said. "I do try to be nice to you, and you never lose an opportunity of speaking unkindly."

Vera laughed, and strolled across to the piano. "I didn't know that was unkind," she said, as she seated herself, and pulled out some music from the rack at her side.

The girl followed her, her hands behind her back; she stood behind her.

"Do you like me, Vera?" she asked.

Vera looked round, and stared at her.

"My dear child," she said, "don't be absurd. I don't dislike you."

"But you do," persisted the other. "I have seen it so often. I've had such convincing evidence, and it makes me a little unhappy." She drew up a chair by the side of the piano and sat down.

"Don't play," she said, "just let us have a heart-to-heart talk."

"That's the kind of talk I loathe. I've just been having a heart-to-heart talk about Quaker oats," said the other. "But this young man, what's his name?"

"Gillingford, Frank Gillingford," said Marjorie, steadily.

"You are rather keen on him, aren't you?"

"I am hoping that he is rather keen on me," said the girl, her sense of humour getting the better of her resentment.

"What is he, an engineer or something?" asked Vera, touching the keys lightly with her sensitive hands.

"Something of the sort." And Marjorie changed the conversation. "Didn't uncle rather, rather", she hesitated for a simile, "as Mr. George would say, 'whack it into' that unfortunate person?"

"You mean the burglar?"

Marjorie nodded.

"I don't think he got any more than he deserved," said Vera.

"Do you really think he came after uncle's collection?

"Why not?" asked Vera, without looking round. "It is a very valuable one. There are medallions there worth three or four hundred pounds each, there is one there worth a thousand, at least," she added quickly. "I believe that is so."

"But what use would they be to him?" persisted the girl.

"Well—" Vera shrugged her shoulders.

"You are asking me to give a psychological survey of a burglar's mind," she said, "and that I am not prepared to do."

Marjorie walked back to the window and looked out on to the dismal landscape. It had been raining for the last hour, and the trees looked especially miserable, half enveloped as they were by a mist which was driving up from the Medway valley.

"I shouldn't advise you to discuss the question of that sentence with your uncle," said Vera across her shoulder. "He is rather sore; I think that was the cause of his quarrel with Hilary George."

The girl made no reply. She could not understand Vera. She had always been an enigma to her. That she was a disappointed woman, Marjorie knew. She had expected to inherit a life of luxurious calm; instead, she had merely succeeded the house-keeper, whom Sir Ralph had thoughtfully discharged, and had, moreover, dated his discharge as from the date of his wedding.

Vera was an ambitious woman. She had set no limit upon her possibilities. She had come, as she had thought, into a wider world, to a larger life, with scope for the exercise of her undoubted genius, but had found herself restricted to the prosaic duties of housekeeping for a querulous and a mean old man.

Marjorie's reverie was cut short by the sudden cessation of the music. There was a little pause, and then Vera's voice asked, "Where could I raise five hundred pounds?"

II — THE CALL OF TILLIZINI

Marjorie turned with a start.

"Five hundred pounds?" she repeated.

Vera nodded.

"I want that sum," she said, "for a purpose. You understand that this is confidential?"

"Oh, quite," said Marjorie, "but it is a lot of money. Couldn't you get it from Uncle Ralph?"

"Uncle Ralph," repeated the other, contemptuously. "He wouldn't give five hundred potatoes! A demand for five hundred pounds would estrange us for the rest of our lives."

She gave a bitter little laugh.

Marjorie knit her pretty brows in thought.

"I can't think of anybody," she said slowly.

"Then don't," said Vera, briskly. "I don't know exactly why I asked you."

Further discussion of the subject was made impossible by the arrival of Sir Ralph himself.

He had evidently forgotten that any strained relations existed between himself and his wife, or that her iniquitous extravagance in prepared oats had ever come between them.

"Vera," he said, going towards her, "did you notice a man in the court to-day, a peculiarly foreign-looking man?"

She thought a moment.

"Yes, there was a person sitting near—" she nearly said Hilary George, but deemed it tactful to mention another barrister who had been engaged in the case.

"How did he impress you?" he asked.

"I should like to say that he did not impress me at all," she said, with a smile. She was most anxious to restore him to good-humour. "But unfortunately, I did take particular notice of him; rather a distinguished-looking man, clean-shaven and with a lined, thoughtful face."

Sir Ralph nodded.

"That's the man," he said. "I've just had a note from him. I didn't know he was in Burboro'. That is Tillizini."

He said this impressively. At the moment, Tillizini's name was in the mouth of half the population of England.

He nodded.

"None other," he said. "I had a note from one of the under secretaries of the Home Office saying that he was coming down. I don't know why our little burglary should have attracted his attention, but at any rate he could not have been very interested, for he did not turn up until to-day. He has just sent a note to tell me that he is staying at the George, and I have written to ask him to come up to dinner to-night."

She made a little face.

"He's a detective or something, isn't he?" she asked.

"More than a detective."

Sir Ralph was rather inclined to be irritable if you did not rise to his values. It was better to over-estimate them than to under-estimate them in any case.

"Surely you have read the papers?" he went on, with his best magisterial air. "You couldn't very well escape his name nowadays. He is the man whom the English Government brought over as a sort of consultant, to deal with this terrible outbreak of crime."

"I've heard something about it," said his wife, carelessly. "The 'Black Hand' or the 'Red Hand', I forget exactly what colour it is."

Sir Ralph frowned.

"You must not treat these matters frivolously, Vera," he said, coldly. "I've had reason to speak to you before on similar occasions. The 'Red Hand' is a very mysterious organization, which is striking at the very heart of our domestic security. Any man, and I may add any woman, should be extremely grateful to those who, by their gifts of divination, are endeavouring to shield the innocent victims of a band of organized criminals."

Vera hated her husband when he made speeches to her. She knew more about the "Red Hand" and its workings than she was prepared to discuss with Sir Ralph.

It was a pose of hers, as it was a pose of certain members of her class, to profess a profound ignorance upon matters which were engaging the attention of newspaper readers. The pose of ignorance is a popular one with members of the leisured classes; popular, because it suggests their superiority to the influences which surround them; because it signalizes their independence of chronicled facts, and because, too, it is the easiest of all poses to assume and to sustain.

Vera had caught the trick and found it a profitable one. It lent her an overpowering naivete, which had a paralysing effect upon the better-informed but socially inferior members of the community, and it precluded one being bored by a long recital of the news which one had read in the morning papers in a more concise or a more accurate form. Her interest in the great Italian detective for the moment was a conventionally domestic one, for she rose from the music-stool.

"I shall have to tell Parker to set another place," she said.

"If he accepts," interjected Marjorie.

Vera raised her eyebrows with a little smile.

"Don't be absurd, Marjorie, of course he will accept."

"What do we call him, Inspector or Sergeant or something?" she asked of Sir Ralph.

The spirit of revolt was stirring within her, and she permitted herself a facetiousness of attitude which ordinarily she would not have expressed. And this, despite the subconscious desire to soothe him into a complaint mood.

She never for one moment imagined that he would advance her the money she required, but he might let her have a portion of it if she could only invent a story sufficiently plausible. The truth was out of the question. She smiled to herself at the thought. She was an imaginative woman but not sufficiently so to picture Sir Ralph in that moment of confession. She needed the money as she had never needed money before. It was not for herself, her own wants were few and her tastes simple. She might, perhaps, induce her husband to let her have a hundred if she could invent a good reason, and it would have to be a superlatively good reason to induce Sir Ralph to part with his money.

Somehow the old weariness of it all, the old distaste for the life she was living, came over her, and induced her to treat the subject in a manner in which she knew her husband would heartily disapprove.

"You will call him Doctor Tillizini,' said Sir Ralph sternly. "He is a professor of anthropology in the Florentine School of Medicine. He is a gentleman, Vera, and I shall expect you to treat him as such."

Marjorie, who had been an interested spectator of the passage between husband and wife, had discreetly withdrawn to her book and her chair by the window. As Sir Ralph turned to go, she rose.

"I say, what fun," she said. "Is he really coming, Uncle?"

Sir Ralph nodded.

"I hope so. I can do no more than invite him, but he is such a busy man that he may probably have to go back to town. At any rate, I am certain," he said, a little pompously, "that he will approve most heartily of my treatment of that rascal to-day. I think it is monstrous the way Hilary George went on..."

He was still sore over his treatment by his whilom friend, and he launched forth into a sea of explanation and justification, and, incidentally, gave the girl a fairly garbled version of the scene which had occurred outside the Session House, a scene in which he had played, by his account, a dignified and proper part, and in which Hilary had lost his temper to a distressing degree.

The fire of Sir Ralph's eloquence burnt itself down to glowerings and splutterings of incoherent disapproval.

"Hilary George," he said, "will regret this." He spoke in the satisfied tone of one who had made special arrangements with Providence to that end.

Marjorie was following her uncle from the room, when a glance from Vera brought her back. The older woman waited until the door had closed behind her husband.

"Marjorie," she said, in the mild and honeyed tone which the girl recognized as her "At Home" voice, "I want you to do something for me."

"With pleasure, dear," said the girl warmly.

Lady Morte-Mannery fingered the little silver ornaments on one of the tables which abounded in the drawing-room, and placed them as though they were pawns in a new game she was playing. She seemed to be concentrating her attention upon this pastime as she spoke.

"I want you to do something very special for me," she repeated. "Of course, I know I can trust you about that money, and now I want to ask you to help me with a little ruse. This man who is coming to-day," she said, "this Italian person, is really not the kind of man I want to meet. I hate detectives and all those crude, melodramatic individuals. They talk about crime and things, and besides," she hesitated, "I can trust you, can't I?"

She looked up sharply.

"Yes," said the girl gravely, wondering what was coming.

"Well, you know, dear," said Vera slowly, and still playing her mysterious game with the comfit boxes and Dutch silver, "I'm a member of a club. It's a ladies' club; you won't find it in Whittaker because we do not care to advertise our existence, although of course we are registered. Well, we had rather a bother there, two or three months ago. We, we. Why should I deceive you?" she said in a burst of confidence, and with her rare smile. "We were raided! You see, dear, we played rather heavily. We did not confine ourselves to the prosaic game of Bridge. Some woman, I forget her name, introduced baccarat, and we had a little wheel too; you know."

She shrugged her shoulders.

"It was awfully fascinating, and one lost and won quite a considerable sum. And then there was a bother, and the police came in one night quite unexpectedly. Your dear Uncle Ralph was in town for the May Meetings, and I had quite a lot of time on my hands.

"It was very fortunate I escaped any serious consequences of my rashness. I gave a false name, and was brought up the next morning at Bow Street with the rest of the women, you remember, the case created quite a sensation, and I was bound over in a false name. Nobody recognized me and nobody but you is any the wiser."

She stopped again, and shot a swift, side-long glance at the girl.

"Oh, you needn't be shocked," she said, the acid in her tone asserting itself. "It wasn't so very dreadful, only this Tillizini man was in court that day, and I think he may have recognized me."

"How awkward!" said Marjorie. "Really, Vera, I'm not a bit shocked, and it's not for me, any way, to sit in judgment on your actions. What do you want me to do?"

"I want you to help me when I tell Sir Ralph that I am too ill to entertain this person. I'll go straight away to bed, and I want you, like an angel, to do the honours."

"Why, with pleasure," said Marjorie, with a little smile.

"Anyway," said Vera, a little hardly, "Ralph won't bully you before visitors, nor will he refer pointedly to your needless extravagance in potatoes. Ralph is rather a fanatic on the question of potatoes," she said. "There is a standard by which he judges all phases of domestic economy."

Marjorie was filled with an infinite pity for the girl. She was not more than seven or eight years older than herself, still young enough to find joy in the colour and movement of life.

"I will do anything I can," she said. For the second time that day she laid her hand upon the other's shoulder.

"Don't paw me, dear," said Vera, with sudden asperity, and the warm, generous heart of the girl was chilled. Vera saw this, and tried to make amends.

"Please don't bother about me, dear," she said, in a softer tone. "I am rather jagged; too jagged, indeed, to meet this—"

At that point the door of the drawing-room was opened, and William, the butler, came in importantly. He stood by the open door.

"Professor Tillizini," he announced.

III — A HUNTER OF MEN

It seemed to Marjorie that Vera shrank back at the name.

The girl waited for her to go forward and greet the newcomer, but as she made no move Marjorie realized that she was called upon, even now, to perform the duties of hostess.

The man in the doorway was tall; he looked taller, perhaps, because of his slimness. He was clad from head to foot in black, and the big flowing tie at his neck was of the same sober hue. He carried in his hand a black soft felt hat, from which the butler had made several ineffectual attempts to detach him.

His face was long and thin, sallow and lined; his eyes were big and grey, and steady. They were terribly alive and expressive, Marjorie thought. They gave the impression that the whole process of life was comprehended in their depths. His hair was black and was brushed smoothly behind his ears. He was neither handsome nor ugly. His face was an unusual one, attractive, because of its very character and strength. The mouth was big and sensitive; the ungloved hands were long and white, and as delicate as a surgeon's.

He gave a quick glance from one to the other.

"I am so sorry to intrude upon you," he said. There was no trace of any foreign accent in his voice. "I expected to find Sir Ralph. He is out, yes?"

He had a quick, alert method of talking. He was eager to the point of anticipating the reply. Before the girl could answer he had gone on.

"He has kindly asked me to dine to-night. I am so sorry I cannot. I must be back in London in an hour or two. There are one or two interviews of importance which I have arranged."

His smile was a dazzling one; it lit up the whole of his face, and changed him from a somewhat morose, funereal figure, to a new and radiant being.

Marjorie noticed that he was almost handsome in his amusement. The smile came and went like a gleam of sunshine seen through a rift of storm-cloud.

"You are Miss Marjorie Meagh," he said, "and you, madam," with a little bow, "are Lady Morte-Mannery." His head twisted for a moment inquiringly. That, and the bow, were the only little signs he gave of his continental origin.

Vera forced a smile to her face. She came forward, a little embarrassed. She had hoped to escape without an introduction and to have developed a convenient headache to keep out of his way.

"I saw you in court," said Tillizini, quickly. "It was an interesting case, was it not? That poor man!"

He threw out his arms with a gesture of pity.

"I do not know why you sympathize with him," said Vera.

"Seven years!" Tillizini shook his head. "It is a long time, Madam, for a man, innocent."

Again the little shrug. The tall man paced the room nervously.

"You have heard his story. He said that he came to this house to meet an individual who would give him a packet."

"But surely you do not believe that?" said the other, with amused contempt.

"Yes, I believe that," said Tillizini, calmly and gravely. "Why should I not? The man's every attitude, every word, spoke eloquently to me, of his sincerity."

"Do you believe, then, in this mysterious Italian?" said Vera.

"Oh, Vera, don't you remember?" Marjorie broke in suddenly, and with some excitement, "there was an Italian in the town. We saw him the day before the robbery. Don't you remember?" she asked again. "A very short man, with a long Inverness cape which reached to his heels. We passed him in the car on the Breckley road, and I remarked to you that he was either an Italian or a Spaniard because of the peculiar way he was holding his cigarette."

"Ah, yes!"

It was Tillizini, tremendously vital, all a-quiver like some delicately strung zither whose strings had been set vibrating by a musician's hand.

"He was short and stout, and was dressed in black," said the girl.

"A moustache, no?" said Tillizini.

The girl shook her head.

"He was clean-shaven."

"You were going the same direction, yes?"

Again the girl nodded, with a smile at the man's eager question.

"And did he turn his face towards you or from you? From you?"

Again the girl nodded.

"He did not want you to see his face?" Tillizini himself shook his head in answer.

"What rubbish, Marjorie!" broke in Vera, petulantly. "I don't remember anything of the sort. There are always organ-grinders with monkeys and things of that sort coming through the village, or ice-cream people who come down from Chatham. You are letting your imagination run away with you." Marjorie was amazed. She remembered now the incident most distinctly. She had spoken of it to Vera in the evening, at dinner. It was amazing that she herself had forgotten it until this moment.

"But you must remember," she said.

"I don't remember," answered the other shortly. "Besides, you are very wrong to give Mr. Tillizini a false clue. There can be no doubt that this man, Mansingham, burgled the house for no other reason than to steal Sir Ralph's collection."

"Instigated by the Italian," said Tillizini. "Oh, you English people," he said, with a despairing shrug, "I am desolated when I speak with you. You have such a fear of melodrama. You are so insistent upon the fact that the obvious must be the only possible explanation!"

He shook his head again in humorous resignation. From any other man the outburst might have sounded as a piece of unpardonable impertinence. But Tillizini had the extraordinary gift of creating an atmosphere of old-established friendship. Even Vera, frankly antagonistic, had a vague sense of having discussed this matter before in identical terms with the man who spoke so disparagingly of her compatriots.

He looked at his watch.

"I must see Sir Ralph before I go back. Where shall I find him?"

Vera had a shrewd idea that at that moment Sir Ralph was engaged in a heated interview with the offending butcher who had put a halfpenny upon the price of beef, but she did not think it fair to her husband, or consonant with her own dignity, to admit as much.

"He'll return very soon," she said.

He looked at her sharply, for no reason as far as she could see. There had been nothing in her tone to justify the look of quick interest which came to his face.

"I have met you before somewhere, Lady Morte-Mannery," he said quickly, "and it is very unusual for me that I cannot for the moment recall the circumstance."

"Really?" said Vera, in a tone which suggested that she had no interest in the matter, "one does have these queer impressions, you'll excuse me now, won't you, doctor," she said, "I have got rather a bad headache and I thought of lying down. Miss Meagh will entertain you till Sir Ralph returns."

He stepped quickly to the door and opened it for her, and favoured her with a little bow as she passed. Then he closed the door and walked slowly back to Marjorie.

"Where, where, where?" he said, tapping his chin and looking solemnly at the girl.

She laughed.

"You must not confuse me with the Oracle," she said. "You know, doctor, we ask such questions of you."

Again that beautiful smile of his illuminated the sombre countenance.

"I was asking this Oracle," he said, tapping his breast. "And now I remember. There was a raid on a gambling house. It was run by one of my compatriots, and I was in court."

"I hope you will forget that, Doctor Tillizini," said Marjorie, quietly. "Lady Morte-Mannery may have been very foolish to have been found in such a place, but it would not be kind to remember—"

She stopped when she saw the look of astonishment on the other's face.

"My dear lady," he said, with his winning smile, "you do not suggest that Lady Morte-Mannery was in any way complicated? It would be wicked, it would be absurd, it would be villainous," he said extravagantly, "to associate such a lady with so sordid a business."

"This was a very commonplace raid," he went on, "they were mostly Italians engaged, and mostly people of very low origin, and my interest in the case was merely the hope of identifying some of the participants as gentlemen who had another interest for me. Lady Mannery was in court, certainly, but she was in court as the guest of the magistrate, Mr. Curtain, the Metropolitan Police Magistrate, who, I think, is some relation of Sir Ralph." This was so, as Marjorie knew. Then why had Vera lied to her? She understood how easy it was for her to make up the story; but why give that as an excuse for not wanting to meet Tillizini?

"There is Sir Ralph," she said suddenly. She had seen the car go past the window. "Do you mind staying here alone, while I go and tell him you are here?"

He opened the door for her, with his quaint little bow. She met Sir Ralph in the hall, and explained the fact that the visitor was waiting.

"Where is Vera?" he asked.

"She has gone to lie down," said Marjorie, "she has a very bad headache."

Sir Ralph swore under his breath.

It was her main weapon of defence, that headache. A convenient, but, to his mind, grossly unfair method of evading her responsibilities. He was more incensed now because he felt that not only had she failed to do the honours of his house towards a man for whose position he had an immense respect, but she had escaped from the just consequence of her carelessness. He had discovered that it was entirely due to her that the extra halfpenny had been put upon beef. She had acquiesced to the imposition in a letter which the butcher had triumphantly produced to vindicate his character.

He was, therefore, at the disadvantage which every man must be, half of whose mind is occupied by a private grievance, when he met Tillizini.

The two men went off to the library for about a quarter of an hour.

At the end of that time they returned to the drawing-room, Tillizini to take his leave of the girl, and Sir Ralph to see him to his waiting fly.

Marjorie saw that the Chairman of the Burboro' Sessions was considerably ruffled. His face was red, his thin grey hair untidy, ever a sign of perturbation. He was, too, a little stiff with his guest.

As for Tillizini, he was the same imperturbable, cool, masterful man. Yes, that was the word which Marjorie sought. This man was masterful to an extent which she could not divine.

"Some day I shall meet you again," said Tillizini, as he took the girl's hand in his own. She was surprised at the strength of his grip. "I would not go so soon, but Sir Ralph has kindly given me permission to see this man, Mansingham, who was convicted to-day."

"I think your labours are entirely misdirected, Professor," said Sir Ralph, gruffly. "You will learn nothing from him but a pack of lies."

"Ah, but lies!" said Tillizini, with an ecstatic gesture. "They are so interesting, Sir Ralph, so much more interesting than the commonplace truth, and so much more informative."

The elder man, who prided himself in post-prandial speeches upon being a plain, blunt Englishman, and inferentially typical of all that was best in an Englishman, had no mind for paradoxes. He grunted unsympathetically.

"You are an Italian," he said. "I suppose these things amuse you. But here in England we believe in the obvious. It saves a lot of trouble and it is generally accurate. You know," he said testily, "these stories of mysterious organizations are all very well for novels. I admit that in your country you have the Camorra, and the possession of that factor probably unbalances your judgment; but I assure you "—he laid his hands with heavy and paternal solicitude upon the younger man's shoulder, "nothing of that sort."

They were standing by the window; the dusk was beginning to fall, and the gas had not yet been lit. He got so far, when of a sudden a pane of glass, on a level with Tillizini's head, splintered with a crash. It seemed to splinter three times in rapid succession, and simultaneously from without came a thick staccato "Crack! crack! crack!"

IV — THE "RED HAND" DRAW BLANK

Sir Ralph felt the whiz of bullets as they passed him, heard the smash of the picture they struck on the opposite wall, and jumped back, white and shaking. Tillizini reached out his hand and thrust the girl back to cover with one motion.

In an instant he was down on his knees, crawling quickly to the window. He reached up his hands, threw up the sash, and leant out suddenly. For a second he stood thus, and then a jet of flame leapt from his hand, and they were deafened with the report of his Browning. Again he fired, and waited. Then he turned, and came back to them, a beatific smile illuminating his face.

"You were saying," he said calmly, "that these things do not happen in England?"

His voice was even and unshaken. The hand that raised a spotless white handkerchief to wipe a streak of blood from his forehead, did not tremble.

"What happened?" asked Sir Ralph, in agitation. "It must have been a poacher or something. Those beggars hate me!"

"Poachers do not use Mauser pistols," said Tillizini quietly. "If you take the trouble to dig out the bullets from your wall, which I am afraid is somewhat damaged, you will discover that they bear no resemblance whatever to the pellets which, I understand, filled the cartridges of your friends. No," he smiled, "those shots were not intended for you, Sir Ralph. They were very much intended for me."

He looked wistfully out of the window.

"I'm afraid I didn't hit him," he said. "I saw him fairly distinctly as he made his way through the trees."

"Who was it?" asked Sir Ralph anxiously.

Tillizini looked at him with an expression of slyness.

"Who was it?" he answered, deliberately. "I think it was the Italian who sent William Mansingham to your house to receive a packet."

"But from whom?" asked Sir Ralph.

"That we shall know some day," replied the other, evasively.

Sir Ralph went down to the railway station to meet Tillizini and to see him off. He was consumed with curiosity as to the result of the interview which he had granted the detective.

Whether he had the right of instructing the warders of the local gaol to admit Tillizini was a moot point; but since the Italian had such extraordinarily wide powers deputed to him by the Home Office, it was probable that the interview would have taken place even without Sir Ralph's permission.

The Chairman had hinted that it would be graceful, if not decent, for Tillizini to see the prisoner in his presence, but the Italian had artistically overlooked the suggestion.

It was five minutes before the train left that Tillizini sprang out of the fly which brought him to the station entrance. He was smoking a long, thin cigar, and was, as Sir Ralph judged, tremendously pleased with himself, for between his clenched teeth he hummed a little tune as he strode through the booking-hall on to the platform.

"Well?" asked the Chairman, curiously, "what had our friend to say for himself?"

"Nothing that you do not know," replied the other, brightly. "He merely repeated the story that he told in the dock about my mysterious fellow-countryman. He gave me one or two details, which were more interesting to me than they would be to you."

"Such as?" suggested Sir Ralph.

"Well," Tillizini hesitated. "He told me that his instructor had informed him that the packet would be small enough to put in his waistcoat pocket."

Sir Ralph smiled sarcastically.

"There are a dozen objects in my collection which might be carried in a man's waistcoat pocket. No!" he corrected himself, "there are at least fifty. By the way," he said suddenly, "you've never asked to see my collection."

Tillizini shook his head vigorously, amusement in his eyes.

"That would be unnecessary," he said. "I know every article you have, Sir Ralph, its size, its origin, almost the price you paid for it."

Sir Ralph turned to him in surprise.

"But how?" he asked wonderingly. "I have only my private catalogue, and no copy exists outside my house."

"Very good," said Tillizini. "Let me enumerate them."

He told them off on his hands, finger by finger.

"Number 1, an Egyptian locket from the Calliciti collection, gold, studded with uncut rubies, value, £420. Number 2, a plaque of Tanagra ware, rather an unusual specimen in a frame of soft gold, inscribed with Syrian mottoes. Number 3, a crystal medallion, taken by Napoleon from Naples, on the inverse side a bust of Beatrice D'Este, on the reverse side Il Moro, the Duke of Milan, value, by the way, I didn't give you the previous value because I don't know it, £600. Number 4, a Venetian charm in the shape of a harp—"

"But," gasped Sir Ralph, "these facts, regarding my collection are only known to me.

"They are also known to me," said the other.

The train had come in as they were speaking. Tillizini walked towards an empty carriage, and entered it. He closed the door behind him, and leant out of the window.

"There are many things to be learnt, and this is not the least of them," he said. "Between the man with the secret, and the man who knows that secret, there are intermediaries who have surprised the first and informed the second."

Sir Ralph was puzzling this out when the train drew out of the station, and its tail lights vanished through the tunnel which penetrates Burboro' Hill.

Left to himself, Tillizini locked both doors and pulled down all the blinds of his carriage. He had no doubt as to the sinister intentions of the man or men who had dogged his footsteps so persistently since he had left London. If he was to be killed, he decided that it should not be by a shot fired by a man from the footboard.

It was a fast train from Burboro' to London, and the first stop would be at London Bridge. He took the central seat of the carriage, put his feet up upon the opposite cushions, laid his Browning pistol on the seat beside him, and composed himself to read. He had half a dozen London papers in the satchel which was his inseparable companion.

One of these he had systematically exhausted on the journey down; he now turned his attention to another. His scrutiny was concentrated upon the advertisement columns. He did not bother with the agonies, because he knew that no up-to-date criminal would employ such method of communication.

One by one he examined the prosaic announcements under the heading "Domestic Servants Wanted." He reached the end without discovering anything exciting. He laid the paper down and took up another.

Half-way down the "Domestic Wants" column his eye was arrested by a notice. To the ordinary reader it was the commonplace requirement of an average housewife. It ran:—

"Cook-General; Italian cooking preferred. Four in family. Fridays; not Thursdays as previously announced. State amount willing to give."

The address was an advertising agency in the City. He read it again; took a little penknife from his waistcoat pocket, and carefully cut it from the paper.

There were many peculiarities about that announcement. There was a certain egotism in the "Fridays, not Thursdays as previously announced," which was unusual in this type of advertisement. Who cared whether it was Thursday or Friday that had been previously given, presumably, as the evening "out"?

But the glaring error in the advertisement lay in the last paragraph. The average advertiser would be more anxious to know what wages the newcomer would require, and would most certainly never suggest that the "Cook-General" whose services were sought, should contribute, in addition to her labour, anything in the nature of payment for the privilege."

Tillizini looked up at the roof of the carriage in thought. To-day was Monday. Something had been arranged for Thursday. It had been postponed till the following day. For that something a price was to be paid, possibly an advance on the original price agreed upon was demanded. The advertiser would hardly undertake to perform the service without some previous agreement as to price.

He did not in any way associate the announcement with the recent events at Highlawn; they were but part of the big game which was being played. The emissaries of that terrible society whose machinations he had set himself to frustrate were no doubt travelling by the same train. He was so used to this espionage that he ignored it, without despising it. He was ever prepared for the move, inevitable as it seemed to him, which would be made against his life and against his security.

It was too much to expect that the "Red Hand" would forgive him the work he had accomplished in America. He had cleared the United States from the greatest scourge of modern times.

It was no fault of his that they had taken advantage of the lax emigration laws of England to settle in the Metropolis.

He replaced the papers in his satchel, and just before the train ran into London Bridge he let up the spring blinds of the compartment. It was dark, and wet, and miserable. He made no attempt to alight at the station. It was not a safe place, as he knew by experience, for a threatened man to end his journey.

There were dark tunnels which led to the main entrance of the station, tunnels in which a man might be done to death, if by chance he were the only passenger negotiating the exit; and no one would be any the wiser for five minutes or so, sufficient time, that, to allow these professional murderers to escape.

Outside Waterloo he pulled the blinds down again. He did these things automatically, without any fear. He took the same precaution as the everyday citizen takes in crossing the road. He looked from left to right before crossing this dangerous highway of his.

Flush with the railway bridge which crosses the river to Charing Cross station is a footpath, Old Hungerford footbridge.

Three men were waiting there at intervals that wet and blusterous night to watch the Burboro' train come in. They saw it from a position which enabled them, had the opportunity presented, of shooting into the carriage.

Tillizini did not know this, but he could guess it. It was not an unlikely contingency.

On the crowded station of Charing Cross he was safe enough. Moreover, there were two men, who had spent the afternoon unostentatiously wandering about the station, who picked him up as he came through the barrier.

He gave one of them a little nod, which none but the keenest observer would have noticed.

The two Scotland Yard men, whose duty it was to shadow him in London, walked closely behind him, and remained upon the pavement outside until he had entered the waiting electric brougham.

V — THE STORY OF THE "RED HAND"

Professor Antonio Tillizini is a name around which has centred the fiercest controversy. No scientist is ever likely to forget his extraordinary paper read before the Royal Society at Sheffield. It was entitled prosaically, "Some Reflections upon the Inadequacy of the Criminal Code," and was chiefly remarkable from the layman's point of view in that the professor in the course of his address calmly admitted that he had found it necessary to kill ten criminals at various stages of his career. He was sufficiently discreet to offer no further information on the subject, and, though his enemies endeavoured, on the clue he had offered them, to bring at least one crime home to the Italian, they were unsuccessful.

More significant of the trend of public opinion, Tillizini was not deprived of his chair of Anthropology at the Florence University, nor did London society bar its doors to the foreigner who was a self-confessed slayer of men.

More than this, it is known that in preparing their Criminal Law Amendment Bill of 19—, the Government sought the advice of this extraordinary man.

But it was in connexion with the remarkable outburst of crime of a peculiar character that the young man who spent six months of the year in England and six months in his beloved Italy, and of whom the epigram had been perpetrated, that he thought in English and acted in Italian, that he first came largely into the public eye.

It was said of him that all the secrets of the Borgias were known to him; there were dark hints amongst the superstitious of necromancy, and this reputation, generally held among the Italian colony in London, served him in good stead when the days came for him to tackle the "Red Hand."

The organization known as the "Red Hand" had been driven from America by the heroism and resourcefulness of Teum, the famous Cincinnati detective. Laws, drastic to the point of brutality, had been instituted; the system of inquiry known as the "Third Degree" had been elaborated so that it only stopped short of the more extreme methods of the Spanish Inquisition, to cope with the increase in blackmail and murder in which the "Red Hand" specialized.

There was a lull in this type of crime after the electrocution of the Seven Men of Pittsburg, but the silence of the "Red Hand" was broken at last.

It was in December, 19—, that Carlo Gattini, a wealthy Italian living in Cromwell Square Gardens, received a curt type-written request that he should place a thousand pounds in banknotes under a certain seat in Hyde Park. The hour and the date were mentioned, and the letter was signed by a small red hand, evidently impressed by a rubber stamp.

Mr. Gattini smiled and handed the letter to the police.

At their suggestion he replied through the agony columns of The Times, agreeing to the request; a package was made up and placed beneath the seat described, and four Scotland Yard men waited through the whole of one dismal evening for the "Red Hand" messenger. He did not come. He either suspected or knew; so there the matter should have ended by the severe and unromantic police code.

But on the following morning another letter came to the Italian. It was brief:—

"We give you another chance. Go to the police again and you are a dead man. Place £2,000 in notes in an envelope and leave it under the first bush in your garden."

In alarm, Gattini went to the police. They pooh-poohed any suggestion of danger. Plain-clothes men were concealed in the house and in the garden; other secret service men were stationed in the house opposite, but again the messenger did not come, nor did the Italian receive any further communication.

On Christmas Eve Mr. Gattini returned from the City after a busy day. He was a widower, and lived alone, save for four servants, an elderly woman who acted as cook, a housemaid, and two menservants.

At 7.30 his valet went to his room to announce dinner. Gattini's door was locked.

The man knocked, but received no answer. He knocked again, without result.

He returned to the servants' hall and announced his failure, and he and the chauffeur went to the front of the house and looked up at the window of Mr. Gattini's room.

It was in darkness.

It happened providentially that a Scotland Yard man had called in at that moment in connexion with the threatening letters, and the servants confided their apprehensions.

The three men went to the door of Gattini's room and knocked loudly. There was no reply, and, putting their shoulders to the door, they burst it open.

One of them switched on a light.

At first they saw nothing; the room was apparently empty... then they saw.

The unfortunate man had been struck down as he sat at his dressing-table. The knife that had cut short his life was missing, but it was evident that he had died without a cry.

This was the first murder, there were others to follow.

The request for money came to Sir Christoforo Angeli, a rich banker, and a naturalized Britisher. He treated the threat as lightly as Gattini had done ... he was shot dead as he stood at his window one Spring afternoon, and no man but he saw the murderer.

Again there came a lull, but it was evident to the police, ransacking Europe for a clue, that the apparent inactivity was less significant of a cessation on the part of the gang, as it was of their successes. Men in terror of their lives were paying and keeping information away from the police. A reign of terror was in progress, when, exhausting the wealthier members of the Italian colony, the gang turned its attention to other sources of income.

Henry S. Grein, a wealthy Chicago broker, and known throughout Europe for his art collections, received the stereotyped demand. He 'phoned the police, and Scotland Yard sent its best man to interview the millionaire at the Fitz Hotel, where he was staying.

"I pay nothing," said the millionaire. He was tall and hard-faced, with a mouth like a rat trap, and the secret service man knew that here the "Red Hand" had come up against a tough proposition. "It is your business to see that I do not get killed; you may make what arrangements you like, but I am going to offer a reward of $20,000 for the arrest of the gang, or the leader."

Then began that extraordinary feud which first opened the eyes of the public to the condition of affairs which existed.

The history of Grein's fight with his assassins on the roof of the Fitz Hotel, his shooting down of the man Antonio Ferrino who had gained admission to his bedroom, the abortive attempt to blow up the Fitz Hotel by dynamite; all these facts are so much history. It was on the morning that Henry S. Grein's body was found floating on the Thames off Cleopatra's Needle that the Government turned to Tillizini.

On the evening of his return from Burboro' Tillizini sat at his broad desk working out a side issue of the problem. The red glow from the shaded lamp by his side gave his face a sinister appearance which ordinarily it did not possess. It was a thin and deeply-lined face, a little sallow and a shade bluish about the jaw and upper lip; the nose was long and pinched, the eyebrows black and arched; but whatever unpleasant impression the somewhat Mephistophelean features may have produced, that impression was forgotten in the pleasant shock which came to the observer who saw Tillizini's eyes.

Italian as he was in every feature, his eyes were almost Irish in their soft greyness; big and clear and luminous, the long black lashes which shaded them gave them an added beauty.

With his left hand resting on his book to keep the stiff volume open at the page, he reached across the table to a gold cigarette box, took a long, thin cigarette, and lit it at the small electric lamp which stood at his elbow.

The room wherein he sat was lofty and spacious. The ceiling and the fireplace were as Adam's magic art had left them. The walls were half panelled in dark oak and, save for a small water-colour sketch of a woodland scene on the left of the fireplace, they were innocent of pictures.

Along one wall ran a bookshelf that stretched from the outer wall to a door near the window.

The windows were long and narrow and were hung with dull red curtains. There was cosiness in the big gilt screen by the fire, in the roomy club chair, the soft thick carpet and the tiny clock that ticked musically over the mantelshelf.

Tillizini read steadily, the smoke of his cigarette rising in blue coils to the ceiling.

Suddenly he closed the book with a snap and rose noiselessly.

He glanced at the clock: it was an idle glance, for he knew the time. He had an eerie sub-consciousness of the hour, be it day or night.

He walked to one of the three windows and looked out upon the Embankment.

He saw a crescent of cold lights that stretched towards Blackfriars and was intersected dimly by the bulk of Waterloo Bridge. Across the river was an illuminated sign imploring him to drink somebody's wine at his own expense; farther down a tall tower of reappearing and vanishing light urged him to the consumption of the only whisky worthwhile.

The professor watched without a smile.

Suddenly a bright splash of light started, and was as suddenly extinguished. Again it flamed, dazzling, white, palpitating light and again vanished.

Tillizini stepped back quickly. From a cupboard he took a strange-looking lamp and a coil of wire. He rapidly affixed the plugged end with a connexion in the wall, then he switched out all the lights of the room, and waited. Again the bright light flickered on the opposite bank.

The professor touched a key at the base of the lamp, and from its conical-shaped projector shot a swift beam of soft blue light.

Twice he did this, when the light on the other bank began to wink furiously and at a breakneck pace. Long wink, short wink, long, short; without a pause it raced onward with its urgent message.

As the lamp spoke Tillizini answered it shortly. He read the message as easily as though it were in a printed book, for he knew English as well as he knew his mother tongue, and, moreover, he was an expert in such matters.

The light on the other shore ceased talking, and Tillizini closed the window at which he had been standing, replaced his projector in his cupboard, and the little table on which it had stood against the wall. Then he drew down the blind and switched on the ceiling light.

He stood over his desk and wrote rapidly the purport of the message he had received. It was written in small cramped signs which might have been, and probably were, a shorthand which he alone understood. He had scarcely finished when the musical thrill of an electric bell arrested him. He pressed an electric push inserted in the leg of the table, hastily slipped his notebook into a drawer, and turned as the door opened.

The neatly-dressed manservant ushered in a visitor.

"Inspector Crocks," he announced.

Crocks was short and stout and jovial. His head was as bald as a billiard ball, his peaked beard was shot with grey; he was a bourgeois of the bourgeois; yet, for all his unpromising appearance, Tillizini had no delusions where this smart policeman was concerned.

"Sit down, inspector", he indicated a chair. "A cigarette?"

The inspector smiled.

"Too subtle for me," he said, "I'm a pipe smoker."

"Fill up," said the professor, with a little smile.

He did not insult his visitor by offering him tobacco, for he knew that it was an attention which all pipe-smokers resent, calling into question as it does their own discrimination and judgment.

"Well?" he asked, as the other slowly filled his polished briar.

"Your countrymen, if you will pardon me, are not helpful, they are a little, er—"

"They are liars," said the young professor calmly. "All men are liars when they are afraid, and I tell you these poor devils are afraid in a way you cannot understand. Not for themselves, but for their children, their wives and their old mothers and fathers." He rose from the table and walked slowly up and down the room.

"These men you want are merciless, you don't know what I mean by merciless. It is a word which to you signifies a certain unjust harshness, cruelty, perhaps. But, my friend... cruelty!" He laughed, a bitter little laugh. "You don't know what cruelty is, not the type of cruelty which flourishes on the shores of the Adriatic. I won't tell you, it would spoil your night's sleep."

The detective smiled.

"I know—a little," he said quietly, puffing a cloud of smoke and watching it disperse with a thoughtful eye.

"Your idea," the professor continued, "is to catch them, very good. And when you have caught them to secure evidence against them, very good again," he said drily; "one is as easy as the other. Now my view is that they are vermin, society's rats, to be exterminated without trial and without remorse."

He spoke quietly; there was no trace of emotion in his voice nor in his gesture. The hand that went searching for a cigarette in the gold box was steady; yet Crocks, no sentimentalist, shivered.

"I know that is your view," he said, with a forced smile, "yet it is not the view which finds favour in this country; it is a view which would get you into serious trouble with the authorities and might even bring you to the Old Bailey on the capital charge."

The professor laughed, a low, musical laugh. He ran his fingers through his grey-streaked hair with a characteristic gesture, then sank into the padded chair by the desk.

"Well!" he said briskly, "what have you discovered?"

The detective shook his head.

"Nothing," he said, "that is, nothing worth while. The gang is unreachable, the people who can give information are dumb brutes; they are either afraid, or in league with the 'Red Hand.' I've tried threatening them; I've tried bribing them; neither is of the least use."

Tillizini laughed softly.

"And the 'Red Hand', have they made any further move?"

The detective's hand went to his pocket. He drew forth a bundle of papers enclosed in an elastic band. From this he extracted a letter.

"This has been addressed to the Sa' Remo Ambassador," he said. "I won't trouble to read it to you; it is the usual sort of thing. Only this time it is a child who is threatened."

"A child!"

Tillizini's black brows met in an ugly frown. "That is their principal card," he said slowly, "I wondered how long they would keep their hands off the children; what does he threaten, our unknown?"

"Abduction first, murder afterwards, if the abduction fails."

Tillizini took the letter from the other's hand and read it carefully. He held the paper to the light.

"This is the American gang, I thought we'd wiped them out, but it was evidently a bigger organization than I credited."

The musical little bell rang overhead. Tillizini raised his eyes, listening. After the shortest interval the bell rang again.

The professor nodded. A big black box stood at one corner of the table, he unlocked it, the detective watching him curiously. With the turning of the key and the lifting of the lid, the front fell away, revealing three sedate rows of crystal phials.

Tillizini took one from the front, slipped it in his pocket, then bent down and pressed the bell in the table.

The door opened to admit a servant, followed by a fresh-coloured young man evidently of the working class. Crocks looked at him, saw he was an Englishman, and wondered in what way the two men had become acquainted. The young man accepted a seat at the invitation of Tillizini.

"Well, my friend," said the professor pleasantly, "you are willing to go on with this matter?"

"Yes sir," said the other, firmly.

Tillizini nodded.

"I got your message," he said. He turned to the detective.

"This man's name is Carter," he said briefly; "he is an out-of-work plumber, unmarried, without family, and prepared to take risks. You have been in the army, I think?" he said.

The newcomer nodded. He sat uneasily on the edge of his chair as though unused to good society, and with obvious embarrassment.

"I advertised," Tillizini went on, "for a man who was willing to risk his life; I'm paying him two hundred pounds, and he is earning it."

Crocks was mystified.

"Exactly what does he do?" he asked.

"That," said Tillizini, with a slow smile, "is exactly what he does not know."

He turned to the other man, who grinned sheepishly.

"I carry out instructions," he said, "and I've had a hundred pounds."

"Lucid enough, Mr. Crocks; he does nothing except live in a lodging in Soho, make his way to a wharf over there," he pointed out of the window, "every evening at about this hour, signal to me a fairly unintelligible message, and afterwards walk slowly across Westminster Bridge, along the Embankment, up Vilhers Street, and so to my house."

He paced the room with long swinging strides.

"He has taken his life in his hands, and he knows it," he said. "I have told him that he will probably be assassinated, but that does not deter him."

"In these hard times," said the soldier, "a little thing like that doesn't worry you; it is better to be assassinated than to be starved to death, and I have been out of work for twelve months until Mr. Tillizini gave me this job."

"He receives two hundred pounds," Tillizini went on, "by contract. I have paid him one hundred, I shall pay him another hundred to-night and his expenses. Probably," he said, with a little smile, "he may escape with minor injuries, in which case I shall congratulate him heartily."

He turned briskly to the man.

"Now let me have all the papers you have got in that pocket. Put them on the table."

The man dived into his various pockets and produced scraps of paper, memorandum, pocket-books, all the literary paraphernalia of his class.

From his pocket Tillizini took the phial he had removed from the medicine chest. He unstoppered it, and a pungent, sickly odour filled the room. With the moist tip of the stopper he touched each article the man had laid on the table.

"You will get used to the smell," he said, with a smile; "you won't notice it after a while."

"What is it?" asked Crocks, curiously.

"You will be surprised when I tell you," said the other. "It is double distilled attar of roses, the vilest smell in the world in its present stage, and this bottle I have in my hand is worth commercially, twenty-five pounds."

At a nod from Tillizini, Carter gathered up his papers and replaced them in his pockets.

"You have a revolver?" asked the professor.

"Yes, sir," replied the man. "I'm just getting used to it. I don't understand these automatic pistols, but I went down to Wembley the other day and had some practice."

"I hope that no occasion will arise for you to have practice nearer at hand," said Tillizini, dryly.

He rang the bell, and the servant came.

"Get Mr. Carter some supper," he ordered. He nodded to the man as he left.

"What is the meaning of this?" asked Crocks.

"That you shall see," said the other.

"But I don't understand," said the bewildered detective. "Why should you give this man so large a sum to do nothing more than send electric signals to you every evening?"

Tillizini sat down at his desk.

"Mr. Crocks," he said, "it would be false modesty on my part if I pretended that my movements escape the notice of the 'Red Hand.' I am perfectly satisfied in my own mind that I do not go in or out of this house without the organization being aware of the fact. Every step I take is watched; every action of mine is considered in the light of a possible menace to the society.

"This society knows that every evening I am engaged in the exchange of messages with a man south of the Thames. The very mysteriousness will naturally appeal to the Latin temperament, and its significance will be magnified. On the second night you may be sure that Carter was located. You may also be sure that he was watched from the wharf and followed to this house."

A light began to dawn upon the detective. "Then Carter is a decoy?"

"A two hundred pound decoy," said the other, gravely. "He knows the risk, I am paying him a big sum; fortunately he is something of a signaller, and so he is able to tell me through a code of our own what is happening on the other side of the river. I freely admit," he smiled, "that so far nothing has happened worth recording."

"They will kill him," said Crocks.

"They will try," said the other quietly; "he is a pretty resourceful man, I think. I am hoping that nothing worse will happen than that they will seek a gentler method of solving the mystery which surrounds him. Hallo!" The door was thrust open suddenly, and the servant flew in.

"I'm very sorry, sir—" he stammered.

"What's the matter?" Tillizini was on his feet. "Is it Carter?"

"No, sir, he's in the kitchen. I heard a ring at the bell, and the girl", he went on incoherently, "a girl sort of fell in. What am I to do, sir?"

"Fell in?" Tillizini stepped quickly past him, and went down the broad stairs, two at a time, to the hall.

The man had had sufficient presence of mind to close the door after the strange visitor's appearance.

Lying on the carpeted floor of the hall was the form of a woman. Tillizini, practised as he was in every subtle move of the gang, stepped forward cautiously. She lay under an overhanging light, and he was able to see her face. He lifted her and walked quickly back up the stairs with his burden.

Crocks was standing in the doorway of the room.

"What is it?" he asked.

Tillizini made no reply. He carried the limp figure and laid it on the settee by the wall.

"What happened?" he asked the man shortly.

"I heard the bell ring, sir," said the agitated servant, "and I went to the door thinking it was—"

"Never mind all that, be brief," said Tillizini.

"Well, I opened the door, sir, and she must have fainted against it. I'd just time to catch her and to drag her into the hall before she went off."

"Did you see anybody outside?"

"No, sir," said the man.

"You closed the door behind you, I see," said Tillizini approvingly. "Really, I shall make something of you, Thomas."

From his medicine case he took a slender phial, removed the stopper, and wetted the tip of his finger with the contents. He brushed this along the lips of the unconscious girl.

"She has only fainted," he said, while with a quick, deft hand he felt the pulse, and his sensitive fingers pressed the neck ever so slightly.

The drug he had given her had a marvellously rapid effect.

She opened her eyes almost immediately and looked round. Then she caught sight of Tillizini's face.

"Don't try to speak," he said, gently. "Just wait. I will get you a little wine, though I don't think you will require it."

She tried to sit up, but his firm hand restrained her.

"Lie quietly for a little while," he said. "This gentleman is a detective from Scotland Yard. You need have no fear."

"Are you Dr. Tillizini?" she asked.

He nodded.

"My husband, you've seen him?" she whispered.

Tillizini nodded again.

"Yes, yes. He was the man who was sentenced at Burboro'."

A look of pain passed across the white-faced girl.

"Yes, he was sentenced," she said, weakly. "He was innocent, but he was sentenced." Tears welled into her eyes.

Tillizini had the narrow blue phial in the palm of his hand. Again he tilted it, and again the tip of his little finger swept across the lips of the girl. She knit her brows.

"What is that?" she said. "It is very sweet stuff."

The professor smiled.

"Yes, it is very sweet, my child," he said, "but it will do you a lot of good."

His prediction was verified, for in a few minutes she sat up, calm and collected.

"I heard you had been to see my husband," she said. "I wanted to talk to you, but you had gone; and then I thought I would write to you, and I was starting my letter when a gentleman came."

"Which gentleman?" asked Tillizini.

"The Italian gentleman," she replied, "the one my husband said had asked him to go to Highlawn. Oh, I knew it wasn't true that he burgled Sir Ralph. Poor as we were, he would never have done such a thing."

Tillizini nodded, he raised his hand with a reproving little smile.

"Yes, the Italian came, and what did he want?"

She was calm again.

"He gave me some money," said the girl, "and told me that he would see that my husband was released, and I was so grateful because I felt so sure that he would go to Sir Ralph and tell him, and George would be let out of gaol."

She was little more than a child, and the men who listened were too full of pity to smile at her naive conception of Sir Ralph's power.

"And then," she went on, "he asked me a dreadful thing."

She shuddered at the thought.

"He asked me to do that for which my husband was convicted."

"To go to the house?"

"Yes," she nodded.

"And to take a package?"

Again the girl nodded.

"And you were to do this on Friday night?"

His eyes were blazing with excitement.

"Yes," she said. "How do you know?"

A little look of fear came into her face. She was out of her depth in these plots and machinations, this simple country girl, who had entered into the responsibilities and trials of marriage at an age when most girls were at school.

"I know," said Tillizini.

He walked up and down the apartment, his hands thrust in his pockets, his head bent.

"You won't be able to do it now. They've watched you come up here; I suppose that's why you came to me?"

"Yes," she said. "I am so afraid of these men. We are quiet country folk. We have never been mixed up in anything like this."

Tillizini considered a moment; then he took down the telephone receiver and gave a number. He had a brief conversation with somebody in Italian and he spoke with an air of authority. He hung the receiver up again.

"I have telephoned for a lady to come here to take you to her house," he said. "I don't think these people will bother you at all, because you know nothing which can possibly affect them one way or the other. I suppose," he said, turning to Crocks, "that you can give me a couple of men to look after this girl till she reaches the house where I am sending her?"

Crocks nodded.

"I'll take her myself," he said, jovially. "I am worth two men."

Tillizini smiled.

"I sometimes think," he said, "that you are worth three. The one you are, the one you can be, and the one you never appear to be!"

Crocks chuckled.

VI — THE THREE

If you walk from London Bridge along Tooley Street, through Rotherhithe, you come to Lower Deptford. Passing through this, you reach Deptford proper, and leading off from the left you will find a long straight road which crosses the Ravensbourne, and connects Greenwich, the one quaint corner of London which steadfastly refuses to be entirely modernized, with its more busy neighbour.

The connecting road once accommodated the well-to-do middle class of Deptford, in the days when Deptford was a prosperous port, and when swarthy seafaring men with gold ear-rings recalled the brave days when the Great Peter himself worked in the shipyard and lived in a piggish fashion at Evelyn House.

The houses are narrow-fronted and of a set pattern. There are overhanging wooden canopies to each of the doors; in some one finds traces of oak panelling, but usually the present-day tenants have utilized such of the wood as they can detach for the purpose of lighting their fires. For what was once Deptford's glory is now Deptford's slum. The great houses ring with the shrill voices of innumerable children. Floor after floor is let out in tenements, and in some cases a dozen families occupy the restricted space which, in olden times, barely sufficed to accommodate the progeny of opulent ship chandlers.

When Mill Lane was Rowtonized, its hovels, its insanitary dens and its quaint little cottages pulled down by a wise borough architect, the Italian colony which had made its home in that unsalubrious neighbourhood moved northward and distributed itself along the road of ancient respectability.

In the main the Italian made a good neighbour, quiet, sober, inoffensive; his piano-organ stalled in the confined area of the back yard, was, perhaps, a nuisance to men who loved to sleep far into the morning, but he gave little offence otherwise.

In one of these houses, on an upper floor, three men were sitting round a table. A large fiasco of Chianti occupied the place of honour upon the table, and glasses had been set for the men by one who was evidently the host. The windows were heavily curtained and shuttered, the door itself had been edged with felt by the careful tenant, and as a further precaution against interruption there sat outside the door, two steps down the narrow stairs, the dark figure of a man, whose duty it was to see that the conference was not disturbed.

The host was a tall man, immensely powerful; his black hair was cropped short; his face, lined and seamed, was half hidden by a bushy black beard.

His shirt opened to show a patch of hairy chest, and the powerful arms revealed by the rolled-up sleeves spoke of enormous strength. They spoke truly, for Tommasino Patti bore in his own country the nickname "Il Bue," which signifies, "The Ox."

It was as "Il Bue" that his companions knew him, though there was nothing bovine in the evil but intelligent face, nor in his lithe, quick movements.

The man on his left was short and stout; clean-shaven save for a black moustache, carefully twisted to a curl at either end. He was short of breath, and spoke like one with chronic asthma, in deep, rumbling, wheezy tones.

Facing Il Bue was a young man who contrasted remarkably with his companions. For, whilst the giant was careless to the point of slovenliness in his attire, and the stout man but little better, this third member of the council was dressed with exquisite care.

He was a slim and graceful young man of medium height; handsome, with his olive skin, his fine forehead, and his slight dark moustache. He wore a suit of simple cut, which fitted him perfectly. His cravat was of dull black silk, and the only jewellery he wore was a black pearl in his cravat, and a thin gold chain across his waistcoat.

He was a man who had been carefully valeted, and, from the dove-grey spats on his boots to his manicured finger-tips, he was correctness personified. His silk-lined overcoat lay carefully folded over the back of the chair, with a soft black felt hat on top. He himself lounged in the one comfortable chair which the room boasted, and his legs thrown over the arm of the chair displayed a glimpse of grey silk socks. He looked little more than twenty, though he was in reality much older.

His attitude towards the others was one of amused curiosity. From time to time he examined his beautiful nails with solicitude, as though he found them much more interesting than the conversation. And yet the talk was startling enough.

The stout man had finished the story of his adventure.

"And Signors," he said appealingly, "I, myself, could have secured this jewel, but for the restrictions which your Excellencies placed on me."

He spoke alternately to Il Bue and the young man at the foot of the table.

"Why?" he asked, in extravagant despair, "why is it necessary that you should employ a third person, one without finesse, like this man, Mansingham, who blunders through the house, awakes the servants, and is arrested? It was tempting Providence, Signors; it would be almost as much a temptation to employ the girl."

The young man smiled.

"You are a fool," he said.

They were speaking in liquid Italian, and the youth's voice was soft and melodious.

"Have we no example of the folly of acting otherwise?"

He raised his eyebrows, and for a moment a baleful light shone in his eyes, changing the whole character of his face.

"Listen, my little man." He tapped the table before him, and spoke with quiet emphasis. "What may seem simple to you is not so simple to us. It is the rule of 'Our Friends,' when such a raid is carried out, that the person who abstracts and the person who immediately receives shall be unknown to one another. Moreover," he said, carefully choosing his words, "it is necessary, since a certain happening which you may remember, that the medallion, if medallion it be, shall be received by two of our brethren, and not by one."

He smiled.

"I repeat," he said, "And not by one."

He looked at Il Bue, still smiling, and then at the stout man.

"A year ago," he said, "we had marked down something we required. It was a medallion. One of those two medallions, I know, contains a secret which will make us rich. We commissioned a brother skilled in scientific abstraction to remove that jewel. It follows, my dear Pietro, that the same set of brains which can wield, with great skill, a set of tools for the removal of locks or the forcing of glass cases may be entirely inefficient or inadequate when it comes to the removal and the safeguarding of the treasure. In stealing, as in all other sciences, the specialist has the advantage; we instruct one specialist to take the medallion from its case, wherever it may be, we employ two other specialists jointly to receive that jewel and to take it to a place of safety, watching each other the while. You follow me?"

The stout man nodded grudgingly, and the young man went on.

"The gentleman," he said, with grim humour, "who received that precious relic of which the society stood in the greatest need, disappeared with it. He was false to his oath, false to his kin; he demonstrated the falsity of the English adage, that there was honour amongst thieves, and indeed there is not, and, although eventually we found him, we never found the jewel."

He took a flat gold cigarette case from his pocket, took out a cigarette and lit it.

"It would have been no satisfaction to us to remove this erring friend. It was fortunate that he saved us the trouble by removing himself. We did not find the jewel," he repeated. "That most desirable thing he had, in his panic, handed to some peasant or other. That peasant we have at last located."

He exchanged a swift glance with Il Bue, and the big man nodded emphatically.

"Whether we shall get the jewel remains to be seen," continued the exquisite young man, puffing rings of smoke at the ceiling.

"At any rate, the necessity for taking precautions in the matter of receiving these articles which are so precious to us, and which are located with such great pains and with such labour, must be fairly obvious."

He looked at his watch.

"Now, I have little time to spare. Let me see what is to be seen."

The big man rose and walked heavily across the room. He put his hand under the pillow of a truckle bed which stood in the corner, and pulled out a long, flat box. He brought it to the other, and opened it with a key which hung with a crucifix about his neck.

It was a curious collection which met the young man's eyes. The box was almost filled with lockets of every conceivable shape and description. There were lockets of gold and of silver, lockets carved from crystal, lockets so encrusted with jewels that it was impossible to tell what was the subsidiary metal. Some bore a painted miniature, others were brilliant with enamels.

The young man fingered them with quick and skilful hands. He lifted them one by one from their box, laid them in the palm of his hand, and turned them; and, as he examined, he rejected.

He finished his labours at last.

"They are very valuable," he said, "but not of the value I hoped. We have to search still further. I believe that the locket which is in the possession of this foolish man Morte-Mannery is more likely to be the one we seek than any other. We must lose no time and spare no pains to secure it."

He took a flat leather wallet from his inside coat pocket, opened it and removed a sheet of paper. There was a drawing in pencil.

"This is it," he said, "if any is."

He passed the design to the stout man.

"You observe those curious arabesques, that cupid, that tiny hoofed devil? That is the master's own work."

He spoke with enthusiasm. For one moment the sinister object of the chase was lost sight of in his artistic appreciation of the design.

"There are two such lockets in the world."

He spoke more quickly now.

"One we may secure to-night. The other on Friday. We must make some arrangements. If necessary I will go down myself and receive the locket. This drawing," he pointed to the paper, "almost decides me. We can afford to slacken our efforts elsewhere and concentrate them upon Burboro'. By the way, what money is wanted?"

"A thousand English pounds," said the stout man, breathlessly.

The young man laughed.

"It is absurd to ask for a thousand pounds for something which may be of no value whatever," he said. "You must promise her, where is she, by the way?"

"She will be in town to-night, Signor," said Pietro.

The young man nodded.

"She is very faithful and enthusiastic," he said; "a curious woman, our Lisa," he mused, as he rose.

Il Bue jumped to his feet and assisted him with his overcoat.

"You will probably find her useful, to-night."

"Why don't you trust her to get the jewel from this pig's house?" asked the tall man gruffly.

The young exquisite smiled.

"My poor man," he said, "if I do not trust a brother, why should I trust—"

"No," he said, a little harshly, as he stood by the door buttoning his coat, "I take no more risks. My father warned me against any such folly, and I neglected his warning. I have had to pay the price for my neglect. Who is outside?" he asked suddenly.

"Beppo," said Il Bue. "I had to have somebody who was reliable. Beppo loves the dark."

"He is an unwholesome beast," said the young man, lightly. "He would cut my throat or yours for a piastre."

"That may be," said the other, with a growl, "but a man whose neck is in danger, and whose life depends upon keeping faith, is one to employ for such work."

They opened the door, the brawny host leading the way, carrying a hand-lamp. A figure sat crouched on the stairs, his knees drawn up and his head bent low.

"A pretty sentry! He's asleep!" said the young man.

Il Bue leant down, and grasped the man by the neck.

"Wake up, you dog," he hissed. "Is this the way?"

Then he stopped, for the head fell back jerkily, and a handle of a dagger protruding from his heart gave them a complete explanation of his silence.

Yes! there he lay, this man, who had perjured himself clear of the scaffold in two countries, this jackal of a villainous confederacy, and the three men stared at him in amazement and horror.

The former state only could be applied to the young man, who, without any pause, without any sign of emotion, continued buttoning his gloves.

"There is only one man who could have done that," he said, thoughtfully, "and that man is Antonio Tillizini."

VII — THE GOLDEN ANTONIO

"Signor, for the love of Heaven!" The Strand was crowded with a matinee throng, and the idle folk which promenade that famous thoroughfare before the Easter holiday filled the sidewalks.

To the man in a hurry the name of the loitering, sauntering pleasure-seekers was anathema. Frank Gallinford was that man in a hurry, for the 6.30 Burboro' express waits for no man, and, though Charing Cross was in sight, there remained only two minutes to get through the crowd, into the station, and on to the platform.

He cursed the idlers deeply and earnestly as he elbowed and pushed his way forward. To leave the pavement was to court disaster, for the roadway was blocked with traffic, and moreover an intelligent authority had had it dug up at its busiest portion and railed off to half its width for "repairs."

Frank Gallinford had stepped from the kerb into the roadway, and from the roadway on to the kerb again, dodging between the hawkers who vended their wares; he had sprung away from the wheels of devastating motor-cars, and buffeted stout and leisurely gentlemen in his effort to reach the station on time, but he seemed as far from his objective as ever.

Then he suddenly felt his sleeve clutched and the words—

"Signor, in the name of Mary!"

They were gasped rather than spoken, and the language employed was Italian.

Frank stopped and looked round with a bewildered frown. Who spoke to him in Italian in this most English Strand, and who knew that he was acquainted with the language?

The man at his elbow was unquestionably Latin. His long, cadaverous face, covered with a week's growth of beard, was working almost convulsively in his agitation. The big black eyes that stared at him from beneath two shaggy brows blazed as only Southern eyes can blaze.

In a moment the Englishman's anxiety to catch his train was forgotten. The soft accents which he knew so well, and loved so well, came to his ears like the first sigh of the breeze that ripples the Adriatic on summer nights. It stirred memories of a simple and charming peasantry, it brought visions of the marble palaces of the old Venetian nobility.

"Well, my friend?" he asked, kindly.

"I cannot speak to you here," said the man, dropping his voice and speaking quickly. "You remember me, Signor? Romano, I was your foreman on the harbour works at Cattaro."

Frank remembered, and his hand dropped in a friendly salute on the other's shoulder.

"Remember you, Miguelo mio!" he laughed, "why, however could I forget you! You were the man who swam out to me when I was seized with cramp, confound you, you saved my life!"

A faint smile flickered across the lips of the little Italian, and then the look of anxiety came again.

"Follow me," he whispered, "this is urgent, you do not know, you cannot understand."

With no other word, he plunged into the throng, and Frank Gallinford, keeping him in sight, followed.

Romano turned the first corner he reached. It was a steep street which led down into the Adelphi.

Here the stream of traffic dried up. Into the gloomy depths only the most experienced travellers, who knew this contributed a short cut to the District Railway station, ventured, and the two men had the thoroughfare to themselves.

When they had gone fifty yards the Italian stopped, and Frank observed that he chose a spot midway between two street-lamps where the light was dimmest and most uncertain.

"Signor," he said, speaking rapidly, almost incoherently, "you know me a little. I am a mason, and I was brought to London to work on the new Italian restaurant in Regent Street. I have no friend in London, no one to whom I can turn, and I am in despair"—he wrung his hands, and his voice, though he kept it low by sheer effort of control, was shrill, "and then I saw your face, your strong, calm English face in that great crowd, Signor, like a saint, Signor...."

Frank was too accustomed to the extravagance of the Italian compliment to feel embarrassed, though he had never overcome the sense of shyness which comes to the more phlegmatic Anglo-Saxon in face of florid flattery.

"I am not feeling particularly angelic, Miguelo," he said, with a rueful smile as the recollection of his lost train occurred to him.

"Listen, Signor," the man went on. "Years ago, when I was younger, I was in New York, and for a joke, Signor, I swear it was no more than a youthful jest, I joined a Society. I took oaths, I thought nothing of it. Then I went away to my own country, later to Montenegro, then to Italy again, and now to London. And, Signor, they have found me, my Society. And they tell me I must do horrible things, horrible, horrible."

He covered his face with his hands and groaned. Frank was puzzled. He knew of these secret societies, had indeed seen their milder manifestations. He had endured an exasperating strike on more occasions than one as a result of some offence given to an official of a society. But never had he glimpsed the tragedy, the underlying horror of these mysterious associations.

He laid his hand gently on the other's arm.

"My friend," he said, soothingly, "you need not worry, this is England. These things do not happen here. If you are threatened, go to the police."

"No, no, no!" protested the man, frantic with terror; "you do not understand. My only hope is to get away ... if I could reach the Argentine, come, come!"

He dragged the other with him to the nearest street-lamp, fumbling in his pocket the while.

"They want me for many reasons," he said, "and for this most of all."

His coat was one of those heavy cloth coats which Italian labourers wear, the corners of the pockets ornamented with tiny triangles of rusty black velvet. From the depths of a pocket the man produced a little case. It looked like a jewel case, and the Englishman observed that it was very new. Romano's trembling hand sought for the catch. He found it after a while, and the satin-lined lid flew open. On a bed of dark blue velvet lay a little medallion.

"San Antonio," said the Italian, in a hushed, eager voice.

It was a beautiful piece of work. The background was made up of small diamonds, the Saint with the Babe was in gold relief. This was no stamped and minted impression, but a piece of rare and delicate carving.

"Signor," said Miguelo, "a month ago a man who was a friend of mine brought this to me, how it came to him I do not know. He asked me to take care of it, and in time, these were his words, Signor, to restore it—"

A motor-car came swiftly down the street, and the Italian looked round apprehensively.

"Take it!"

He thrust the case into Gallinford's hands, clicking it close as he did it.

"But—"

"Take it, ah!"

The car drew up abreast of them and, as the lacquered door swung open, Romano shrank back against the railings.

Two men alighted, and they were followed by a woman.

She was tall, slim, graceful. Frank could not see her face, for it was thickly veiled, but her voice was low and sweet.

"This is the man," she said, and pointed to the cowering Italian.

The two men sprang at Romano and caught him by the arms. There was the click of handcuffs.

"What is the meaning of this?" asked Gallinford, though, with a sinking heart, he anticipated the answer.

"This man has taken a jewel of mine," the lady replied.

"What does she say, what does she say?" asked the Italian. The conversation had been in English; Frank translated.

"It is a lie, a lie!" screamed Romano, struggling desperately as they dragged him toward the car; "save me, for God's sake, Signor!"

The Englishman hesitated. He had all the national repugnance of a "scene." He knew that the Italian would at any rate be safe at the police station, and if he were guilty, as it seemed probable, he needed no protection. The whole story was a cock-and-bull invention.

"Where are you taking him?" he asked.

"To Marlborough Street," said one of the men gruffly.

"Go quietly, Miguelo," said Frank, turning to the struggling man, "I will follow you."

But the prisoner had gone limp, he had fainted.

They lifted him into the car and the men jumped in after. The woman waited expectantly. Then Frank saw a second car behind. As the first car manoeuvred to turn, he heard voices in altercation. Miguelo had recovered from his swoon; there was a scuffle, and the Italian's head appeared at the window.

"Signor!" there was agony in his voice, "tell Signor Tillizini—"

A hand was placed over his mouth, and he was dragged back as the car rolled up the hill and into the slow-moving traffic.

Frank waited. He half expected the woman to speak. Then it occurred to him that she would regard him, if not as an accomplice, at least as a friend of the arrested man, and he went red.

She stepped lightly into the second car. This did not turn, but made its way downhill.

It was on the point of moving off when he remembered with a shock that, if he was not the thief, he was all unwillingly a receiver. The jewel was still in his pocket.

The car was on the move when he realized this and sprang to the door of the carriage.

"Madame," he said, "a word, I have something to say, I have—"

Through the open window of the car he saw the woman draw back.

"I want you—" he began, and jumped back as he saw the flash of descending steel.

He was just in time.

The thin stiletto aimed at him struck the edge of the window, and Frank, temporarily dazed, stumbled to his knees in the muddy road as the car jerked ahead and vanished round the corner of Adam Street.

One glimpse he got of a white hand still clasping the hilt of the quivering poignard, a white hand on a finger of which glowed a square black opal.

He rose slowly to his feet, dumbfounded. He was furiously angry. She had evidently mistaken him for a robber.

He brushed the mud from his knees with a handkerchief, and collected his thoughts, swearing softly.

Here was he, a prosaic young engineer on his way to meet his fiancee in prosaic Burboro', engaged in an adventure which was three parts melodrama and one part comedy.

"This comes from listening to plausible Italians?" he said, savagely. He made his way to the Strand and hailed a taxicab.

"Marlborough Street Police Station," he directed.

He would rid himself of this infernal jewel and clear himself, at any rate.

The sergeant returned his greeting curtly, taking in the mud-stained figure with professional suspicion.

"Romano," he said. "No, we haven't a Romano here."

"He has just been arrested by two of your men," said Frank.

"No warrant has been executed for a man of that name," said the sergeant, shaking his head. "Just wait a minute and I'll ask Bow Street."

He went into an adjoining room, and Frank heard the tinkle of a telephone.

By and by the officer returned.

"Neither Bow Street nor Vine Street know anything about it," he said.

Briefly the young man told the story of the arrest, omitting only the fact that the jewel reposed in his pocket. He had no desire to find himself detained. With Miguelo to confirm his story and with the prosecutrix present to identify the jewel, it would be different. And he had, too, an overpowering desire to explain to the murderous lady, in person, his honourable intentions.

"No sir," the sergeant went on, "we've no Italians, we've had enough of them since the 'Red Hand' started operations in England. But since Mr. Tillizini began working for Scotland Yard, they haven't been so busy."

"Tillizini?" cried Frank, with a start.

The sergeant nodded.

"That's the gentleman," he said, complacently; "if you want to know anything about Italian criminals, you'd better see him—108, Adelphi Terrace; anyway, you'd best come back again, the C.I.D. men may be working independently."

Frank walked in the neighbourhood of the station until ten o'clock that night. He sent a wire to his host and dined at a Piccadilly restaurant.

The clock was striking the hour when he again mounted the steps of Marlborough Street Station.

The sergeant was not alone. Three over-coated men were talking together in one cormer of the room.

"Here he is," said the sergeant, and the three turned and surveyed the young engineer gravely.

"What was the name of that Italian you were inquiring about?" asked the sergeant.

"Miguelo della Romano," replied Frank. "Have you found him?"

The officer nodded grimly.

"Picked him up in the Embankment Gardens, an hour ago," he said.

"Where is he?" asked Frank.

"In the mortuary," said the sergeant, "with twenty-five knife-wounds in his body."

VIII — THE RARE COLLECTION

Marjorie Meagh sat at breakfast with her uncle.

Sir Ralph was in an unusually irritable mood. Breakfast was never a pleasant meal for him, but his fault-finding was generally concentrated upon the domestic shortcomings of his wife and the quality of the food.

Now they took a wider range. He put down his paper suddenly and savagely.

"I wish to Heaven Vera wouldn't go dashing off to town," he said.

Although he was a domestic tyrant of a common type, he stood in some little awe of his young wife. On three occasions in their lives she had startled him by the vehemence of her rebellion, and with every explosion he had grown less self-confident and less satisfied with his own capacity for commanding the situation.

Marjorie looked up from her letters.

"Vera is making a serious study of the drama," she said. "You must remember, uncle, that if by any chance she does succeed as a playwright it will mean an immense income to her."

She was very tactful. She knew that monetary considerations influenced her uncle. It was Vera's career, which she had discovered two years before, when a little play, written for a charitable entertainment, had met with recognition at the hands of the critics.

Though it had pleasantly surprised her husband to the possibility of his having discovered a self-supporting wife, it had been also a source of constant irritation to him. It meant expense, constant visits to the Metropolis, the cost of seats at a theatre, though this latter expense had happily been spared him of late by the discovery of a relation engaged in newspaper work, who had provided complimentary tickets.

But it meant opening the flat in town; it meant the detachment of a servant from a household where the domestic arrangements, as planned by Sir Ralph, were so devised as to fully occupy every moment of the time of every person engaged.

Sir Ralph took up the paper only to put it down again a moment later.

"That scoundrel, Mansingham, has appealed," he said. "It is monstrous."

The institution of the Court of Criminal Appeal was a sore point with Sir Ralph. He felt that its creation had been expressly designed for the purpose of annoying him. He had written letters to Times about it, and had expressed himself, at such public functions as gave him opportunity, in no gentle terms. It was remarkable, under the circumstances, that the Court of Appeal continued to sit.

"It is monstrous," he said again. "It is a slight upon the men who are engaged in carrying out the work of administering criminal law."

His anger came in little spasms. He had a fresh grievance every few moments. Again his paper came down after an interval.

"That young man, Gallinford, did not arrive last night, Marjorie," he said, severely. "The young men of to-day seem to be lamentably deficient in good manners."

"He wired, uncle," protested the girl. "He said that he was detained in town."

"Bah!" snapped her uncle, "that isn't good enough. I am a man of the world, Marjorie. These flimsy excuses do not suffice for me, and I advise you, if you desire to be happy, and the only way to be happy," he said parenthetically, "is to be without illusions, to view these unsupported excuses with suspicion. He is a young man," he went on, elaborating his grievance, "newly arrived in England after a long absence in a barbarous country—"

"In Italy, uncle," she murmured, "it isn't exactly barbarous, is it?"

"Barbarous?" he said explosively. "Why, here are two Italian murders in one day!" He flourished the paper in support of his contention.

"Of course it is barbarous! And he comes back to civilization after a long absence, to a beautiful girl, and I admit that you are that, Marjorie," he said comfortably, with an air of one who was partly responsible for her beauty, "and instead of rushing, as he should, and as young men did in my day, to his fiancee, he breaks his journey in town! It is perfectly inexcusable!"

She did not defend her lover. She knew how valueless such arguments were with her uncle. He was entirely without inclination to reason, at breakfast-time, at any rate.

For the rest of the meal he grumbled spasmodically behind the paper. He reminded her irresistibly of a dog with a bone. From time to time he fired little sentences at her, sentences which had neither beginning nor end, and were generally associated with the Government's shortcomings.

Suddenly she heard the grind of carriage wheels coming up the carriage drive, and jumped from the table. She gave one glance through the window and, without a word to her uncle, flew from the room.

He glared after her in astonishment. In a few minutes she came back, with a delicate flush on her face and laughter in her eyes, leading a tall, broad-shouldered young man, brown of face and smiling a little uneasily, for he did not contemplate the coming interview with any great sense of joy.

"This is Mr. Gallinford, uncle," said the girl. "You have met him before, haven't you?"

Sir Ralph not only had met him before, but did not wish to meet him then. He was in no mood for introductions to strange people. He had, moreover, a grievance against this young man who had so slighted his hospitality. He greeted Frank Gallinford with a grunt in which he expressed in his bluff, hearty English way, as he imagined it, at once his welcome and a foretaste of the reprimand which was coming.

"I am glad to meet you, sir," said Frank.

He held out a big, hearty hand and shook Sir Ralph's.

"I owe you an apology for not having come last night."

Sir Ralph inclined his head. There was no doubt whatever about the apology being due.

"I had a little adventure," Frank went on, and proceeded to relate the chief events of the previous evening.

In spite of the fact that he had made up his mind to accept no explanation as being adequate, Sir Ralph found himself listening with keen interest. The girl's face showed her concern.

"Oh, Frank," she said, in a shocked voice, "how terrible! Was he killed?"

Frank nodded.

"I had an interview with the famous detective, what is his name?"

"Tillizini?" said Sir Ralph.

"Yes," said Frank, "that was his name. A remarkable chap. Of course I handed the locket over to the police, and Tillizini has it now."

"It's very extraordinary," said Sir Ralph, with a puzzled frown. "Your description of the locket sounds very much like one I have in my collection."

A sudden panic of fear passed over him. What if this was the famous locket? What if it had been abstracted without his noticing it?

"Excuse me," he said.

Half-way to the door he turned. "Will you come along with me? perhaps your description of the medallion may be useful. I have got a fear—"

He shook his head.

"You don't think it's yours?" said the girl.

"I don't know," said Sir Ralph. He was obviously agitated. They followed him from the room to his study, a handsome combination between that and the library. From a steel drawer in his desk he took a key and led the way again upstairs.

Sir Ralph was more than an amateur collector. Whatever his judgments might be on the Bench, there were few who could dispute his knowledge of those articles of virtue which it was his delight to collect. The Morte-Mannery collection, though a small one, was famous. It was Sir Ralph's pleasure, from time to time during the year, to show his treasures to the great connoisseurs of Europe.

The joy of possessing something which nobody else had, or if they had, only in a minor degree and in a less valuable form; and, moreover, to hold these wonders of dead craftsmen which were coveted by less fortunate people, and which is the basis of every true collector's pride, was the great passion of Sir Ralph Morte-Mannery's life.

He had devoted forty years to securing and arranging the hundred and fifty lockets which formed his collection. The room in which they lay had been specially constructed with a view to resisting fire and burglars.

It was an open secret that, in rebuilding Highlawns after he had acquired it, the whole scheme of renovation had circled about the collection room. It was more like a prison than a museum, thought Frank, as he followed his conductor through the narrow entrance guarded with steel doors faced with rosewood.

It was lighted by a large window, heavily barred, and the glass itself being set with strong steel network. Burglar alarms of the most ingenious character rendered entrance without detection almost impossible. Floors, wall and roof were of reinforced concrete. One long case ran the length of the room, a strip of carpet on each side forming the only attempt that had been made at comfort. The cases themselves were under heavy wooden shutters, and these Sir Ralph unlocked.

It was a disappointing display to the average man. Row after row of medallions, dull gold, silver, jewels, enamels. There was nothing to excite the enthusiasm of any other than a connoisseur.

Very quickly, one by one, Sir Ralph unshuttered the cases, his anxious eyes running over the neatly-ticketed rows.

"No," he said, after a survey, "nothing has gone. I thought from your description that my Leonard...."

The fire of the enthusiast came to his eyes. With hands that shook a little he unlocked one case, and lifted out a small gold medallion.

"Why!" exclaimed Frank in astonishment as he took it in his hand, "this is the very locket which the man gave me!"

Sir Ralph smiled.

"That is impossible," he said. "Impossible! Only two such lockets were known, and one has been irretrievably lost." He held the little jewel in his hand gingerly. "This and its fellow were made by the greatest artist that the world has ever known, Leonardo da Vinci. The date is probably 1387, and the design is Leonardo's own. It expresses something of the master's genius. As you know, he was a man who was not satisfied with painting pictures; there was no branch of art, from sculpture, to the very mixing of paint, in which he did not interest himself. He was a doctor and a chemist of no mean qualities, and it was after the great plague in Milan in 1386 that he made the two lockets, of which this is the only one extant.

"One he gave to his patron, Il Moro, the usurper of the Duchy, and the other he gave a year or two subsequently to Caesar Borgia. They were both commemorations of his patron's escape from the plague. You will observe on the back", he turned the jewel over gently, "there is an allegorical representation. You see the picture of the little fiend?", he pointed it out with his little finger, "that represents the sickness which visited the whole of Italy. You see the angel? that must represent his 'unconquerable patrons.' What the other signs are—" he smiled, and this cheerless room saw all the smiles that Sir Ralph was prepared to bestow upon the world, "are incomprehensible to me. Probably Leonardo was a Futurist."

He chuckled at his own harmless jest, and the girl listened to him wonderingly, for he was a different man in this atmosphere. She had never seen him so before; he was human, and tender and keen.

"The other medallion," Sir Ralph went on, "was stolen from the Dublin museum. The thief was traced, after a great deal of trouble, to a cross-Channel boat; he was seen to go on the boat to cross from Harwich to the Hook of Holland. There must have been some of his confederates on board, for in the night a great outcry was heard in one of the cabins, and the detective who watched him saw him fleeing along the deck pursued by two foreigners. Before they could either arrest the men who were following or capture the man himself, he had leapt overboard, and with him, it was presumed, had passed the second medallion."

"What was the meaning of it all?" asked Frank.

Sir Ralph shook his head.

"We don't know. It was supposed at the time that he was endeavouring to give the jewel to some of his confederates, and that in the act of doing so he was seen. The men who were chasing him that night on the ship gave a plausible explanation; they said they thought he was mad and endeavouring to commit suicide, and they were trying to prevent him."

He turned the jewel over again, and looked at it lovingly before he replaced it in its case.

"Whatever it was your unfortunate man had," he said, "it was not the fellow to this." Outside, he was himself again, cold, hard, commonplace, but that little glimpse of his true character revealed much to Marjorie.

She understood now the ferocity of the sentence he had passed upon Mansingham. His collection was more than wife or child, more precious than ambition; his passion was strong enough to override his sense of justice.

He looked at his watch with a frown. He had remembered one of the unpleasant facts of life.

"Vera has not returned. I thought she would have come down by the same train as you."

"I was the only passenger for Burboro', as far as I can remember," said Frank.

Sir Ralph looked at his watch again.

"There's another train in by now," he said, "she ought to be here."

He had hardly spoken the words when Vera's voice was heard in the hall below, making inquiries of the servants.

"Oh, there you are," she cried.

She looked up as the party descended the broad stairway into the hall. For a moment a look of wonder came into her eyes at the sight of Frank.

"You have never met Mr. Gallinford, have you?" asked Marjorie, as she introduced them.

"I am very glad to meet you now, at any rate," said Vera, cheerfully.

She was glad, too, that there was some other interest to temper her husband's annoyance. That he should be annoyed she took for granted. It was the atmosphere which invariably met her on her return from town.

He looked again at his watch and then at her, and she understood the significance of the examination.

"I am so sorry," she said, carelessly. "I lost the fast train and had to take the slow one. It was very annoying. I think my watch must have been wrong."

Vera had a very beautiful voice, low and rich, and full of beautiful qualities.

"You've been seeing our wonderful collection?" she said.

Sir Ralph snorted. He hated any claim to partnership in respect to his medallions, and Vera knew it. It was her oblique reply to his unspoken attack.

"You haven't seen the best of them; you ought to see the belts," she said.

"That is a collection which is not sufficiently complete," interrupted Sir Ralph stiffly, "to be examined. Really, Vera, I wish you would not embarrass me by these references."

He strode off to the library, leaving them alone.

She laughed softly.

"He's a great trial sometimes," she said, half to herself.

Then she turned to the girl, and Marjorie noticed with pleasure that the moodiness and depression of yesterday was entirely dissipated. She was at her brightest, her ready smile came and went.

In a few moments she was chatting with Frank Gallinford about Italy as though she had known him all her life.

"It must be a quaint country," she said. "You know, I've a peculiar affection for the land, I am half Italian myself."

"Are you really?"

It was Marjorie who asked the question with girlish delight. "Oh, I say, how romantic! Don't you ever want to stab uncle with a stiletto or something?"

She laughed, but Frank's smile was a trifle grim. He had too vivid a recollection of somebody striking at him with a stiletto to derive the full amount of amusement out of the question. That was part of the story which he had not deemed it necessary to tell.

"Oh, no," drawled Vera, "I never feel sufficiently bloodthirsty."

Suddenly Frank's face went drawn and grey. He stepped back with a little cry.

"What is the matter?" asked Marjorie, in alarm.

He passed his hand over his eyes.

"But really, aren't you ill?"

He shook his head.

"No, it's a little passing giddiness," he muttered. He was seized with an over-powering anxiety to get away.

"I forgot," said the girl, sympathetically, "you've had such a trying night. I'll see if your room is ready; perhaps if you were to lie down for an hour or two you would be better."

He nodded, and, raising his head, met Vera's curious eyes.

"If you will forgive the impertinence," he said, slowly, "that is a curious ring of yours."

She turned white and put her hands quickly behind her back; but too late, he had seen the square black opal, for the second time in twenty-four hours.

IX — COUNT FESTINI

"Why, Miss Meagh, how perfectly delightful!"

Marjorie turned with a start. She was leaving Victoria Station, and had stopped at a bookstall to buy a few magazines.

She had been visiting Ida Mansingham, the wife of the convict, who was in a nursing home. She had had a bad nervous breakdown, and it was due to the generosity of George Hilary and Tillizini that she had been placed in comfort.

A young man was standing before her, his white teeth showing in a smile of sheer delight.

"How extraordinary! I have not seen you for two months. Where have you been hiding?"

She offered her hand with some embarrassment. Her last parting with Count Festini had been such that it seemed that they could never meet again on terms of commonplace friendship. His passionate declaration still rang in her ears. He had come to Ireland for the hunting, had fallen, so he declared, hopelessly in love with her, and had declared his passion.

He had stormed and raved when she had gently refused him; yes, this well-bred and perfectly-mannered young man had behaved more like a madman than a sane product of twentieth century civilization.

And here he was as though nothing had happened.

"I tried to find where you were," he said.

His eyes had the tender softness of the South. His voice was without any trace of foreign accent. He was, as usual, she observed, faultlessly dressed, with none of the ostentation or errors in taste which so often in the foreigner mar the good tailor's best efforts.

"I have been away in the country," she said, a little hurriedly.

She was expecting Frank at the station. He might come up at any moment. She wondered what would be the effect on this volcanic young man if she introduced the big Englishman as her fiancé.

"And I have been tied to town," he said. "Oh, what a deplorable place London is for those whose business keeps them there! It is delightful to the visitor, to the dilettante, but for the unfortunate dweller by compulsion, terrible."

He threw out his hands in mock despair.

"London is a bad habit," he went on, "and the ideal one, for it is a bad habit one can get away from when one likes."

"Few bad habits are like that," she smiled.

He had apparently completely recovered from his infatuation and was genial only to a point of correctness.

Some thought occurred to her, and she smiled.

"Do I amuse you?" he said, with a twinkle in his dark eyes.

"I was thinking," she said, "how curious it is that I seem to have met nothing but Italians, to have lived almost in an atmosphere of Renaissance the last few days."

His eyes steadied.

"That is very curious," he said, quietly. "I could have almost said the same. And who are the Italians who have been favoured by association with the most lovely lady in England?"

She raised her hand.

"Please," she said, softly, "let us forget."

"I could never forget," he said.

He spoke calmly enough for her ease and comfort.

"But I have agreed myself to forego hope. After all," his shoulders rose imperceptibly, "one cannot have all the things one wants in this world. I have most of them, yet one which is more than all the others together, is denied me. That is my punishment."

He smiled again. "But you did not answer me."

She hesitated. She had no wish to talk of Tillizini. He was one of those mysterious individuals engaged in a business of such a character that it seemed that any reference to him would be a betrayal. She saw the absurdity of this view almost as quickly as she formulated the idea.

"One of them," she said, "was Professor Tillizini."

His cigarette was half way to his mouth. He checked its course for the fraction of a second.

"Signor Tillizini," he drawled. "How very interesting. And what had the great Antonio to tell you? Did he ask for your finger-prints, or take a sample of your blood, or express any desire to measure your head?"

"Oh, no," she said, with a laugh. "He didn't do anything so dreadful. Do you know him?"

"Slightly," he said, carelessly. "Everybody in Italy, of course, knows Tillizini, and I should imagine almost everybody in England is similarly informed. And where did you meet this great man?" he bantered.

"At Burboro'," she said. "He came to visit my uncle."

"At Burboro'?"

Again she noticed the slight emphasis to his words.

He was looking at her steadily, speculatively, she thought. He was quick to realize that his attitude was a little more than disinterested, for he gave a short laugh.

"You think I am inquisitive, do you not?" he said. "But don't you know that everything associated with you has immense interest for me? You see," he said, apologetically, "I have never met your uncle. I didn't know that you had such a relative, though most people have. At any rate, I have discovered where you are staying," he said, with laughing menace. "I have only to run to ground this uncle of yours, and the rest will be easy. I shall come to Burboro'," he threatened, with one slim finger raised in mock earnestness, and go round asking 'Has anybody seen Miss Marjorie's uncle?' It will create a little sensation, will it not?"

"I will save you that trouble," she smiled. "My uncle is Sir Ralph Morte-Mannery."

"Oh, indeed," he nodded his head. "I thought it might be."

"Why?"

"Well, you know, he is a great man; one hears of him. He is a judge; and something of a collector, too."

She had seen a tall form walking towards them, and went pink again.

"I want to introduce you, Count Festini," she said, "to my fiancé, Mr. Frank Gallinford."

She averted her eyes from his face, and did not see the sudden tightening of his lips, nor the curious, quick droop of his eyelids.

"This is Count Festini," she said.

The big Englishman put out his hand, and grasped the other's heartily. He was almost head and shoulders above the dapper young man, but, to Frank's surprise, it was no soft, effeminate grasp which was returned. It was a grip which reminded him of the vice-like grip of Tillizini's.

Frank was a typical Englishman, tall, broad-shouldered, lean of face and limb; grey, honest eyes shone with pleasure to meet a friend of his beloved.

"I wish you would bring us just a handful of your beautiful Italian sunshine, Count," he said. "In this city of gloom, and depression, and inquests—"

"Inquests?" interrupted Marjorie.

Frank nodded.

"Yes, on that unfortunate man who was murdered. I have got to give evidence to-day."

"Which man is this?" asked the Count, interested.

"The man who was found in the Embankment Gardens."

"Oh!"

It was only an ejaculation, but Frank looked at him in surprise.

"Did you know him?" he asked.

"I only know what I have read in the papers," said the other, calmly. "May I ask, Mr. Gallinford, exactly what part you played in that tragedy?"

"I was the man that was with him when he was kidnapped," said he. "I have felt awful ever since. If I could only have kept with him I might have saved his life."

"Or lost your own," said the Count. "These people are not particular to a life or two. You have lived long enough in my country to realize that we do not place the exaggerated value upon human life that you Northerners do."

"You cannot have an exaggerated value on human life," said Frank, gravely. "It is the most precious thing in the world."

The Count shrugged his shoulders.

"That is a point of view," he said. "It is not mine. For my part I regard life as the least valuable of our possessions. It is a huge gramophone record on which all the strident and unpleasant sounds of life are received and held at one and the same time. And the whole makes a tremendous discord," he said, speaking half to himself. "The music of life is drowned, overwhelmed, deadened by the harsher notes of strife and ambition. For me," he smiled, "I think that the clean record is best."

"What is the 'clean record'?" asked Frank.

"Sleep," said the other, a little bitterly, "or death. It is one and the same."

He offered his hand with a charming smile.

"I am keeping you both," he said. "Where may I have the pleasure of seeing you again, Miss Meagh?"

"I shall be staying with my uncle for another month," she said.

He nodded pleasantly to Frank, and, turning, walked quickly away. He stopped at a little cigarette kiosk on the station, and watching them out of the corners of his eyes, he saw that they were passing slowly from the station. He turned, when they had disappeared through one of the exits. His face had no longer that pleasant, soft quality which had distinguished it a few minutes before. It was hard and set, and his eyes glowed angrily. He stood watching the exit through which they had disappeared, then he went to a telephone box. From this he emerged in five minutes, collected, suave and cheerful.

It was Thursday, the night before the attempt would be made. If the locket was not abstracted, he thought he knew a way by which it might be attained, and it was a pleasant way to him. The only fear he had in his mind was whether he would resist the temptation which would arise in the experiment. Whether his love of gain would over-master the growing passion which fired his breast for this cold, beautiful Englishwoman.

He had learnt enough now to know that the second locket was in the possession of Tillizini. It was a house which, under ordinary circumstances, might be burgled; but now it was Tillizini's. The name inspired awe amongst the lawless men who were working for their illicit profits.

Before now the very sight of this professor's thin, refined face had stayed the assassin's dagger, from very fright. The very mention of Tillizini was sufficient to cause a stir of uneasiness amongst these villains, in whom the dictates of fear and pity were dead.

But the name had no such effect upon Count Festini. He was superior to fear of any man. He came from a line of men who, for hundreds of years, had dominated one secret society or the other. The Festinis went back to the bad old days of Italian history, when assassination was a quick and easy method of ridding members of his family from embarrassment.

It was in his blood. It was part of his composition. Young as he was, he had been the directing force of the terrorizing organization which had worked the Eastern States of America into a ferment of terror.

Tillizini, swift and terrible in his working, wise in his judgment, had broken that organization.

Festini was no fool. He had recognized that the game was up in America. There was no use in running his head against a brick wall. He had foreseen the possibility of transplanting the strength of his government to England. They were a soft people, used to crime of a certain type, crime which was generally without violence. It was the last stand of the "Red Hand." Its members had been driven from every country in Europe. It was only a matter of time when lethargic England would drive and stamp the organization out of existence.

But, in that short space of time, Festini was preparing his coup, the greatest and most terrible of his wicked plans. He would strike, not individuals, for that was too dangerous, he would blackmail the nation, but first he must obtain possession of those lockets.

He sprang into a cab outside the station, and drove to a little street in Soho. It was a tiny restaurant where he knew he would find Il Bue. There was no time to be lost.

The man he sought had not arrived, and the Count sat down and waited, ordering a plate of soup from the obsequious head-waiter.

The big man came in shortly afterwards.

"Talk in English as much as you can," said Festini.

"The man is a brother," replied the other.

"That does not matter," said the Count. "Talk in English, if you please. You have sent your men to Burboro'?"

The other nodded.

"You have followed my instructions?"

"Yes, fair one. The men I have sent looked like Englishmen. They are the best we can get."

"Trustworthy?"

The other nodded, and smiled crookedly.

"As trustworthy as men could be who are up to their eyes...." He gave a significant little gesture, and Festini smiled a little.

"I don't think we shall have any difficulty," he said. "When you get the locket, bring it straight to me. You will be at the station to receive them. Take it from their hands; do not leave the station until you have it in your hand. I shall be waiting for you at Deptford. Now, what of Tillizini?"

A look of fear came into the big man's eyes.

"Tillizini?" he said, uneasily.

"Yes," said the other, impatiently. "What do you fear? He is only a man, my Ox. One of the lockets is in his possession. It is in that big room of his that overlooks the Thames Embankment. Now, can that be secured?"

The big Italian shook his head vigorously.

"Signor," he said, earnestly, "it cannot be done. There is not one of our men who would dare to. You know he is no man, this Tillizini, he is a devil. Remember Beppo Ferosti! Only the other night, killed on the stairs, by a man who heard all we said. And we none the wiser! It is not possible, Signor, to trap this man. We have tried.

"Did we not try in New York?" he went on, vehemently. "We bribed the waiter of his hotel, we drugged him, we went to his room at night and dragged him out of bed, wrapped him in a sheet and threw him down the elevator shaft. Signor, he dropped eight stories," he said, impressively, "and when we went later to see him at the bottom, it was not him at all. It was poor Antonio Barricci, the man who had been in charge of all the arrangements, who had planned his death. We had not seen his face in the dark, because we dared not carry lights. We simply took the drugged form from the bed and carried it to the elevator shaft.

"Do you remember how we sent the man from Florence to kill him? We never saw that man again," the big man's voice shook a little, for the man from Florence had been his brother. "Tillizini sent me his hand, that is all, by parcel post! Just the hand of the man from Rome, with the rings of the brotherhood still upon his finger. No name to identify the sender, and the postmark 'Paris.'

"It cannot be done, I tell you," he said, "the man is not human."

Festini was listening with an amused smile.

"He is sufficiently human, my friend," he said, softly, "only he is more clever than the men who have been pitted against him. Now I propose, myself, to arrange matters with Signor Tillizini. I have tried every one of our agents, and they have all failed. I must take up my share of the work. Here is a dangerous enemy, who may spoil our plans. To-night, whilst our friends are reconnoitring the ground at Burboro', I myself will work independently."

"Shall I come with you?" asked the other, eagerly. "Signor, I would give my life for you."

He spoke with sincerity. There was no questioning the honesty of the dog-like faithfulness of this big man.

Again Festini smiled.

"I will work alone, my good friend," he said, and tapped the other on the shoulder with his white hand, approvingly. "These things must be done with subtlety if they are to succeed."

He rested his head upon his hands for a few minutes, deep in thought. The other waited patiently, his deep-set eyes filled with love and admiration for the master whose house he had served all his life.

"There is a man," said Festini, suddenly, "who is a sort of agent of this Tillizini. Now, you shall go to him and kill him."

He spoke as though it were a very ordinary transaction which he had asked the other to undertake.

Il Bue nodded.

"It will be simple," he said. "I can do it to-night."

Festini was still thinking.

"No," he said, after a while, "do not kill him. Take him away to the house by the river. You know where I mean?"

The other nodded.

"When you have got him safe, send a letter to Tillizini saying that you have him, and demanding a ransom, say of 500, and leave the rest to me."

The big man rose.

"I will see about this at once, Signor," he said. "God prosper you."

With which commendation he left the restaurant.

X — A WAY OF TILLIZINI'S

Tillizini was sitting in his room, examining a number of photographs that he had received that morning from Florence, when the note came to him.

He opened and read it.

It was brief and to the point.

"We have taken your spy. You will give us five hundred English pounds, and he shall be released. By Order of The Red Hand."

He folded it carefully.

"Is the messenger still waiting?" he asked.

"No, sir," said the servant, "it was a boy who handed it in."

Tillizini examined the note again, and smiled. He rose from the table and went to the telephone which stood on a small bracket near the wall. He gave a Treasury number which is not in the telephone book, it is only to be found in the small volume issued to Cabinet Ministers and to public officials, and in a few seconds he was connected with Inspector Crocks.

"They have taken my man," he said; "at least they say they have, and I suppose they are speaking the truth. They demand £500 for his immediate release."

"What are you going to do?" asked the inspector's voice.

"I'm going to release him," said the other, "though I have my doubts as to whether they really want the money."

In a few minutes they were driving to Smith's lodgings. The landlady gave him all the information he required, and another hour's search revealed the place where his man had been captured. As he thought, it was on the wharf from whence he usually set his make-believe flash-signals. There were signs of a little struggle. Some children, playing in the dark street from which the wharf was gained, had seen four men, very drunk as they thought, staggering to a waiting motor-car.

There is a little club in Soho where men, with certain political views, may be found between the hours of eleven at night and five in the morning.

At a quarter to twelve the stout man Pietro, who had formed the third at the Deptford conference, entered the club and, after a fruitless inspection of its members, came out again.

He walked through Soho, crossed Oxford Street, and entered one of the slummy thoroughfares which abound in the neighbourhood of Tottenham Court Road.

He let himself into a gloomy house with a key, and closed the door behind him.

His room was on the ground floor. He unlocked the door, went in, and again closed and locked it before he struck a match.

His hands were fumbling with a match-box when there was a quick, blinding flash, and he found himself standing in a circle of light thrown by an electric light.

"Don't move," said a voice, "or I will kill you."

The intruder spoke in Italian.

"You may light the gas," said the unknown.

The circle of light followed the alarmed man, as he moved to the centre of the room, reached up and ignited an incandescent burner.

"Tillizini!" he gasped.

"It is I," said the other easily. "Your doors are shut, yes. Your windows are shuttered, of course. Sit down."

Shaking in every limb, the man obeyed. The revolver in the professor's hand was an excellent excuse for obedience.

"Where have you been to-night?"

"That is no business of yours," growled the other. "You have no right to come into my room. What have you stolen?"

"Don't be foolish," said Tillizini, calmly. "Stand up again, put your hands above your head. Thank you, Signor."

His deft fingers searched the other, removed a revolver from the hip-pocket and a knife from inside the waistband of his trousers. These he laid on the table, first jerking open the chamber of the revolver scientifically. There was a little clatter of cartridges as they fell on the floor.

"Now I want your hand," he said. "Hold it out."

Hesitatingly, the other man obeyed, his fearful eyes fixed upon the calm face of the other.

Tillizini leant over and raised the hand to his face. His sensitive nostrils dilated. He had no difficulty in detecting the scent of the attar of roses with which his spy's papers had been impregnated.

"Yes," he said, "you are the man I want."

The fear deepened in the stout man's eyes.

"What do you mean?" he gasped.

He had a superstitious dread of this undefeatable man. With the ignorance of his kind he had endowed him with powers which were almost supernatural.

"I want the man you helped to kidnap to-night, or if you did not help to kidnap, assisted in searching," said the Italian, pleasantly.

"It's a lie," said the other. "I know nothing about a kidnapped man."

"The man you searched to-night," continued Tillizini, unemotionally, "whose pockets you ransacked, whose papers you examined. Where is he?"

The look of fear in the man's face was ludicrous.

"How do you know?" he gasped.

"I know," said Tillizini. "That is sufficient."

He waited for the stout man to speak, but in whatever fear he stood of the detective, his terror of reprisal from his comrades was a greater factor.

"I can tell you nothing, nothing," he said, sullenly.

"Then you shall come a little journey with me," said Tillizini. "We will leave the light, if you don't mind. Get up."

He went to the door and, standing with his back against it, unlocked it.

"You will go first," he said.

Outside the street was deserted, save for a number of children who were playing noisily in the roadway.

"To the right," said Tillizini, curtly.

The man obeyed.

Drawn up by the opposite side of the pavement a little way along was a pair-horse brougham. Opposite this Pietro waited till Tillizini's voice stopped him.

"Get in."

Again the man obeyed and Tillizini followed. He closed the door, and the prisoner noted that he gave no instructions as to where the man was to drive. Evidently that had already been arranged. His wonder was dissipated when he found the carriage driving along the Thames Embankment. He was going to Tillizini's house. He pulled himself together. He was half losing his nerve. After all, Tillizini could not torture him here, in the heart of London, and he a Government official.

It was to Adelphi Terrace that the carriage drove and pulled up before the detective's house.

"Get out."

The map followed his instructions. Tillizini's ring was instantly answered by a servant. The two men stepped into the hall.

"Has anybody been?" asked the detective, in English.

"No, sir, except a man called with a parcel for you."

"A parcel?" He looked thoughtful. "A large parcel?" he asked, idly.

"No, sir, a smallish parcel," replied the man. "He would not leave it until I signed for it."

"I see," said the detective, "and so you left him at the hall door whilst you went down to get a pencil?"

The man smiled.

"Oh, no, sir, I took the parcel from him, there it is on the hall table. I wouldn't leave the door."

Tillizini's lips twitched. In the most tragic moments of his life he could find sources of amusement. He scarcely gave the parcel more than a passing glance. Instead, his eyes rapidly surveyed the floor. He opened the door, and looked at the lock. It was a patent lock with a small catch. From the slot into which the bevelled snap caught he extracted two little threads. He examined them briefly and kept them between the finger and thumb of his left hand. All the time he kept his hold upon his revolver, though the servant did not observe it.

"Very good, Thomas," he said, as he closed the door again, "you may go. Marchez, mon ami."

This last was to his prisoner. Pietro obeyed. He mounted the broad staircase to the dark landing above, and Tillizini stepped close to his prisoner.

"Go through that door," he said.

Pietro did so.

He flung the door open, hesitated a moment, then stepped in. When the Italian's hand was on the knob of the door, Tillizini spoke. He was addressing apparently a person below.

"All right, Thomas," he said loudly, "you may bring up that parcel now."

Then he pushed Pietro into the room. It was in complete darkness, as he expected. The captive stood hesitating in the doorway for a fraction of a second, Tillizini behind him, waiting. He had only to wait for an infinitesimal space of time. From the darkness in the room four shots rang out in rapid succession and Pietro pitched forward on his face, a dying man.

Tillizini had moved swiftly under cover of the doorway. He offered no view of himself to his hidden enemy. He heard the quick steps of Thomas. In the hall below were governing switches by which any room in the house could be illuminated. A quick order from Tillizini, and the lights blazed up in his room.

He sprang in, leaping over the twitching form of the fallen man. The room was empty; it offered no cover to any person in hiding. There was no need to search beyond the open window. The man who had waited there had already prepared and carried into effect his escape.

Tillizini shut down the switch and the room was in darkness again. He flew to the window. A slender rope had been fastened to the leg of his heavy writing table. It extended across the room, through the open window, and now swung to and fro in the breeze below.

The street was empty. There was no profit in searching farther. He closed down the window and 'phoned the police.

The man on the floor was too far gone for help. He was dying when Tillizini reached his side. With the help of the servant and a hastily-summoned policeman he was laid on the settee, where a few nights before the helpless and innocent victim of the "Red Hand's" plotting had lain.

Tillizini's busy hands plucked phial after phial from his medicine chest... the man revived a little, but it was evident, long before the police surgeon came, that he had no chance. He looked up at Tillizini's emotionless face with a faint smile.

"Signor," he said, in Italian, "I ought to have known better, it was thus you trapped others. I have certain monies at the bank", he named the institution, "I wish that money to go to my sister, who is a widow at Sezzori."

"That I will send, Pietro."

"You know my name," said the dying man.

"I know you very well," said Tillizini.

The man looked at him bleakly.

"Someday," he said, at last, his voice was growing fainter, "they will have you, our brave 'Red Hand,' Signor, and there will be a great killing."

He checked himself and looked round at the uncomprehending policeman, who could not understand the language, and at the servant, obviously English and agitated by the extraordinary character of the evening.

Then he half whispered.

"There is something I wish to tell you, Signor."

His voice was now difficult to hear. Tillizini bent his head to catch the words, and in that moment the dying man mustered his last reserve of strength; by sheer effort of malignant will he called into play all the vital forces which were left alive within him. As Tillizini's head sank lower and lower, Pietro's hand crept to his side.

"Signor," he whispered, "take that!" Quick as he was, Tillizini was quicker. As he whipped round, his vice-like grip held the other's wrist, and the gleaming knife fell with a clatter to the polished floor. Then with a quick jerk he flung the man's hand down on the settee and stood up, smiling.

"How like a rat, Pietro, how like a rat!" And the dying man, unrepentant of his many villainies, of the sorrow and the suffering he had brought to so many people, saw with the glaze of death filming his eyes, the lips of Tillizini part in an amused and contemptuous smile.

An hour later Tillizini sat in the private office of Inspector Crocks, of Scotland Yard.

"It was a narrow squeak for you," said the inspector, admiringly.

"There were two," said Tillizini, dryly. "Which one do you mean?"

"The first, I think, was the most serious," said the Englishman.

"Now it's strange that you should say that," said Tillizini. "I think the second was, the dagger was poisoned. I discovered that soon after."

"Poisoned?"

"Yes, with a poison that is not a particularly pleasant one, tetanus," he said.

"Good God!" said the inspector, genuinely shocked. "That's the germ of lock-jaw, isn't it?"

Tillizini nodded.

"That is it," he said, cheerfully. "A pleasant end especially planned for me. I tell you these men are scientists in a crude way. I knew he was upstairs waiting, the first man. An old trick that, you've probably had it played on innocent suburban folk of this city hundreds of times."

The inspector agreed with a gesture.

"When the amiable Thomas closed the door, our friend who delivered the parcel quickly put up a piece of canvas paper backed with a strong silk fabric. The door caught in the staple, but so did the strong silk. When he considered the coast was clear and he judged Thomas to be out of the way, he had but to pull the projecting end—"

"I know the trick," said the inspector. "I've seen it done a score of times."

"I suspected something of the sort," said Tillizini, "but mostly I suspected a parcel. I thought, too, that the kidnapping of Smith was a ruse to get me out so that a warm welcome might be prepared for me when I came back."

"Have you found the man?"

"He'll be found," said Tillizini, "by to-morrow morning."

"I've got men out now hunting for him," said Crocks. "It's rather a difficult job, Tillizini, dealing with your people."

Tillizini smiled.

"They are somewhat different to the average English criminal," he said. "One of these days when you are in Florence, Inspector, you must come to my museum and I'll show you the skulls of typical criminals of all countries. I will explain then to you just why our Southern men are more dangerous to handle, and if you would be patient with me," he favoured the policeman with his little bow, "I would then as briefly as possible give you the basis by which you may forejudge men's actions."

"In other words," said the Inspector, jovially, "you'll give me elementary lessons in necromancy."

"Something of the sort," said Tillizini. He had had half an hour with Crocks and with the Commissioner. Another crime had been laid at the door of the "Red Hand." A worrying business for the English police, however satisfactory it might be to Tillizini.

He rose from his chair and looked at his watch; it was nearly twelve. The inspector followed his example.

"Where are you going now?"

"I'm going back to my house," he said, "will you come?"

"I have an hour to spare," said the other, "and I like your room, it's rather restful. If I shan't be in the way I'll come round and get a few particulars at first hand."

"Come along," said Tillizini.

He passed through the broad corridors of Scotland Yard, down the stone stairway, and out by the entrance near the arch. The policeman on duty at the door saluted him respectfully.

They strolled together leisurely back to the house in Adelphi Terrace. Tillizini rang; it was an act of laziness on his part that he did not find his key. There was no reply, and he rang again. Then he opened the door himself and stepped in. The two hall lights were burning, but there was no sign of Thomas.

Tillizini closed the door behind him. Thomas was usually to be found in the basement. He walked to the end of the passage and called over the stairs, but again without reply. Neatly folded on a little dumb waiter, placed for better security beneath a glass, was a note. Tillizini pulled it out, took it up and read it. It explained much. It was addressed to the man, Thomas.

"I have been arrested in connexion with to-day's crime," it said; "please bring my overcoat at once to Bow Street."

It was signed, "Antonio Tillizini."

Without a word he handed the wire to the English detective.

"We will now go and discover things," he said, and led the way upstairs.

He did not trouble to arm himself because he knew the ways of the "Red Hand" too well to believe that any of the organization were present. They had probably had half an hour after Thomas had hurried away with the necessary overcoat. They would do what they wanted to do in ten minutes.

He opened the door of his room and walked in without fear. He switched on the light. The room was in confusion. There had been a diligent and damaging search. The drawers of his desk had been ripped open and the floor was covered with papers and splinters of rosewood.

Not even the chairs and the settee had escaped attention. They had been cut open and their stuffings pulled out. The legs of one chair had been lopped off as by a machette. Strangely enough, the little case of medicines, which still stood open on his desk, had been left intact. The "Red Hand" had too great a respect for Tillizini's knowledge of chemistry, and they had had such illuminating lessons of his knowledge of high explosives, that they had left this severely alone, excepting that there was plenty of evidence that each phial had been carefully and cautiously lifted from its velvet-lined well and examined.

With a quick glance at the damage done, the Italian walked with rapid strides across the room, lifted up one corner of the carpet and slipped back a narrow panel in the floor. It had been cunningly constructed by Tillizini's own hand. It would be almost impossible for anybody not in the secret to know that such a receptacle existed. He thrust in his hand, and felt for a little while with a grim smile, then his hand slowly withdrew. The detective saw that he held a paper.

"For the locket, thanks," he read; "now you shall hear from us, Tillizini."

The Italian said nothing. He stood in the middle of the room, his hands clasped on his breast, his head sunk in thought.

"They have taken the locket," said Inspector Crocks, aghast.

Tillizini did not reply.

There came a knock at the door, and Thomas, still with his master's overcoat on his arm, entered.

"I'm sorry, sir; did you?" he began.

Tillizini raised his head.

"Thomas," he said, "I have told you under no circumstances must you leave this house. Your failure to carry out my instructions, however, is mainly my fault. To-morrow I will draw you a little sign which you will see on any letter or wire I send, and know that it comes from me."

"I'm very sorry, sir," said Thomas. Tillizini waved his apologies away.

"It is nothing," he said, "all this; rather," he smiled, "I owe you an apology. You have a little child, have you not?"

"Yes, sir," said Thomas, wonderingly. "You carry his portrait in a locket, do you not?"

"Oh, yes, sir," replied Thomas. "Why, you know I do, sir. I brought you the locket to see the other day."

"I am sorry to say, Thomas," said Tillizini, gravely, "that I have lost it, I hope it may be recovered. I put it in a safe place, I assure you."

"Oh, it's nothing, sir," said Thomas. "I can get another. It wasn't worth half a crown."

"A token of a father's love is invaluable," said Tillizini, the corners of his lips turning up.

He took his revolver from his pocket, pressed a spring near the trigger guard, and a little silver lid flew open in the butt. He held his hand under it and shook it, and something fell out wrapped in silver tissue. He unrolled the paper and handed the contents to Crocks.

"I am almost inclined to ask you to keep this in Scotland Yard," he said, "yet I don't think they will burgle me again."

It was the medallion!

"As for that which they have stolen," Tillizini went on, "it is regrettable. I feel I shall never forgive myself for losing that charming locket of yours."

His voice was filled with gentle mockery, and the servant grinned a little sheepishly, mumbling his depreciation of any fuss at so small a loss.

"I'm not at all annoyed, sir," he said, awkwardly.

What was true of Thomas was not true of the two leaders of the "Red Hand" who at that moment were sitting in a little room in Deptford examining with consternation and chagrin the plump and smiling features of a healthy child of two.

XI — LADY MORTE-MANNERY HELPS A FRIEND

Sir Ralph Morte-Mannery was in an amiable mood. He had just read a most complimentary reference to his own perspicacity and genius in a French journal devoted to the interests of collectors. His gaiety had affected the other members of the little dinner party, and had tempered somewhat the natural annoyance of the quashing of George Mansingham's conviction.

That unfortunate man had been released, not because the judges of the Appeal Court thought that his sentence was excessive, but because, in summing up, Sir Ralph had outraged most of the canons of good taste which it is possible for a judge to outrage.

In giving judgment their lordships had said many bitter things about Sir Ralph; indeed, so unkind had been some of their comments, that Hilary George, listening with that air of delighted wonder which was his normal attitude toward life, had felt a sinking of his heart as he thought of the humiliation which by his efforts he had brought upon his sometime friend.

Hilary was too good a man and too good a sportsman to exult in his victory. He was a strong man, too. None but a strong man would have taken the first train to Burboro' and carried the news of the result to a man who would consider himself as being almost within his legal rights in slaying the messenger.

There had been a stiff little meeting in the library; later, something like a reconciliation. Hilary, in terms which his old friendship permitted, gave the result of the finding, toning down the more vigorous of the judges' remarks, and inwardly praying that The Times, in its record of the case, would sub-edit it as mercifully.

Sir Ralph had been prepared for some such upset. He himself was an excellent lawyer where his prejudices did not interfere with his judgment. The lawyer in him had told him that his sentence had been excessive, just as the collector in him demanded as emphatically that the man should have been hung. But Hilary, with his baby face and his babbling humour, and his readiness to laugh at jokes against himself, had broken down the reserve of the older man, and had been invited to stay on.

Over the dinner-table Sir Ralph even drank his health in facetious terms. The host's humour was not of a great quality. But it was quite sufficient, as indeed it is in the case of all men whose flashes of humour are few and far between. He insisted on referring to Hilary as the "enemy" or "my oppressor," and it gave him considerable amusement to do so.

"Now, Hilary," he said, with heavy jocularity, "you must give us all the news of the best criminal circles. What are the 'Red Hand' doing? Really, they are killing as many people as the motor-buses."

"Those people who know best," said Hilary, gravely, "are viewing the inactivity of the 'Red Hand' with some apprehension. I happen to know the Government is rather worried about it. These men are brilliantly organized, and they will stop at nothing."

"Has anybody discovered," asked Marjorie, "why they are rifling the collections? There was an article in the Post Herald about it the other day."

Hilary shook his head.

"I'm blessed if I can understand it," he said, "there's something behind it. I don't want to bother you, Ralph," he went on, "but doesn't it ever strike you, as a lawyer and as a man of keen perceptions, that there really might have been some 'Red Hand' move behind that burglary of yours?"

Sir Ralph shook his head.

"I shouldn't think it was likely; of course, it might be so," he conceded graciously, though in his heart of hearts he was perfectly satisfied that it was nothing of the sort.

"Their latest exploit," said Hilary, "was to kidnap one of Tillizini's agents. The man was taken away overnight and turned up whole and hearty in the morning. For some reason they'd given an order for his release, being, I think, under the impression that they'd killed Tillizini and there was no necessity to retain his agent. The man could give very little account of his movements, except that he had been more or less stupefied by the administration of a drug which somewhat dulled his powers of recollection. He was unable to assist the police in locating the house where he had been taken. He was found in a dazed condition sitting on one of the seats on London Bridge in the early hours of the morning, and has been in a more or less semi-conscious condition ever since."

"That's very interesting." Frank, who was seated next to Marjorie, leant across the table. "I've seen men like that in Italy; it's a sort of opium preparation that some of the peasants take. There is a slang term for it in Italian, an abbreviation of non mi ricordo."

"He remembers nothing, any way," said Hilary, "except—" He stopped.

"Except what?" asked Vera.

She had been a silent listener to the conversation. She was looking very beautiful to-night, Hilary thought. She wore a dress of grey chiffon velvet, one big pink rose in her corsage.

"I forget now," said Hilary. He remembered that he had received his information in confidence and that he himself might be associated in the case at a later period.

"By the way," he went on, "I saw you in town the other day."

Vera reused her delicate eyebrows.

"Really," she drawled, "that was awfully clever of you. Where was I?"

"You were in Oxford Street," said Hilary. "That was an awfully swagger motor-car you were driving in; was it Festini's?"

She looked at him steadily.

"Festini?" she repeated.

"I thought I saw you with Festini," he said hastily.

For a man with such a wide knowledge of human creatures and, moreover, so versed in the ways of society, he seemed to be making an unusual number of faux pas.

"I do not know Festini," she said, "if you mean Count Festini, whose name one sees through the medium of the public press as moving in exalted circles; nor have I ever been in a motor-car in Oxford Street since I drove with Sir Ralph to Buzzard's last Christmas."

"I am sorry," murmured the barrister.

Vera changed the subject with an easy grace. She was a perfect hostess, though she required all her self-control to prevent her showing the anger she felt.

"Go on telling us something about the 'Red Hand'," she said. "What is this immense coup one hears about? I am awfully keen to know."

"Nobody seems to have any information on that subject," said Hilary, "not even Tillizini."

"Not even Tillizini?" she repeated in mock amazement.

"Not even Tillizini," repeated Hilary. "He seems to be as much in the dark as any of us."

"People are getting a little jumpy," said Sir Ralph, as, at a signal from Vera, the two women rose from the table. "There was another article in this morning's paper. I know the journalists who are generally behind the scenes in these things expect something pretty big to happen. The police are guarding all the public buildings, and every Cabinet Minister is being shadowed with as much care as though the 'Red Hand' was a suffragist organization."

The party laughed politely at Sir Ralph's little gibe.

"I can confirm that," said Frank, as he selected a cigar from the box which Marjorie offered him. "The various corporations responsible for their safety have asked a number of engineers to make an inspection of the bridges."

"Across the Thames?"

He nodded. "There's a water-guard every night for these," he said; "all the signs are pretty ominous."

Sir Ralph and Hilary strolled away. They were both interested in the collection, and Vera joined the other two.

"I am not going to stay long with you," she smiled; "don't look so alarmed, Mr. Gallinford."

She was genuine in her desire to propitiate him. His attitude towards her was a little strange and stiff. If she knew the reason, she gave no indication. In a way, he amused her. He was so open and so English. She experienced the resentment of her remote ancestry stirring within her at his dogged, unwavering honesty. Her attitude to the distress of Marjorie was at once polite and antagonistic. She, Marjorie, had remonstrated with him without effect. With all her pride in her lover, she desired that he should stand well with others and should inspire in them the same admiration which she herself felt for him.

Vera's attempt at conciliation on this occasion was crowned with no greater success than her previous effort. After a while she yawned slightly behind her hand. She apologized laughingly.

"Do not think you poor people are boring me," she said, "but I've had some rather trying nights lately. Where are you going?" she asked.

"I am going into the billiard-room to play Marjorie a hundred up," said Frank, with an heroic attempt to be genial.

Vera nodded.

"And I've got my accounts to bring up to date."

She made a wry little face. "Pity me," she demanded, with a smile.

"Can I help you, dear?" asked Marjorie.

Vera shook her head.

"Accounts," she said, with thinly-veiled acrimony, "are mysteries into which I trust your future husband will never initiate you."

With a nod she passed out of the room. She returned a few minutes later as though she had left something behind, and found the room empty. She made her way to the billiard-room; the game had just started, so they were settled for at least half an hour.

She looked at the jewelled watch on her wrist; it wanted five minutes to ten. She came back to the hall and went up the stairs slowly, and as slowly walked past the museum. The iron door was closed, but its rosewood covering stood ajar. Ralph was engaged in an argument on the respective values of Renaissance artists which would last for at least an hour. She quickened her steps. At the other end of the corridor her own room was situated. Highlawns had been reconstructed to suit Sir Ralph's convenience. In a sense it was convenient to her too, for she had chosen a small room in a wing which was never fully occupied unless Sir Ralph had an unusually large house-party.

She closed the door behind her and locked it. It was a pretty room, furnished with taste, though it contained little that could by any stretch of imagination be termed valuable. Sir Ralph had his own views on the luxury of the age, and the simplicity, not to say the meanness, of his domestic arrangements, was a concrete expression of his disapproval of modern luxurious tendencies.

The room possessed, what is unusual in English country houses, long French windows which opened on to a balcony. She looked at her watch again, then drew a heavy curtain across her door. The gas was burning dimly. The room might have been a sitting-room but for the big white bed which stood in an alcove, screened from view by thick silk curtains.

She did not trouble to turn up the light. She looked at it for a moment in doubt, and then walked to the window. Again she looked at the light hesitatingly, and, walking back, turned it out. She opened the window and stepped out on to the balcony.

It was a mild, pleasant night. The moon was hidden behind a bank of clouds, but there was sufficient light to distinguish the more prominent objects in the big, sweet-smelling garden below. She looked carefully left and right, and saw nothing. She went back to her room to get a rug, and resumed her vigil. The clock of the village church had struck ten in its lugubrious tones when she heard a slight sound in the garden below.

She walked back to her room quickly, opened a cupboard, and took out a silk ladder; there was a hook attached, and this she fastened with deft fingers to a socket in the balcony, fixed in the wall, ostensibly to support the sunblinds when their cover was necessary.

She dropped, the ladder over. A dark form rose from the shadow of the portico beneath and mounted the swaying cordage. He leapt lightly over the balustrade, and stopped for a moment to pull up the ladder after him, and to lay it on the floor of the balcony.

She took his hand and led him into the room, closed the windows, shuttered them, and pulled the velvet curtains across. Then she lit the gas and returned to him. She laid her two hands upon his shoulders, and looked hungrily into his face.

Beautiful as she was, the love which shone in her eyes transfigured her face and intensified her loveliness.

"It is you!" she breathed. "Oh, thank you for coming yourself! I was afraid that you would send one of those wretched men of yours."

Festini smiled kindly. He patted her cheek caressingly.

"I had to come," he said, "though it is not long since I saw you."

"It is two days," she said, reproachfully.

He nodded.

"So it is," he smiled. "You got my letter?"

For answer she took a crumpled envelope from her breast.

"You ought to bum that," he said, half seriously. "It is a very dangerous thing to keep letters, even though they are apparently innocent.

"You have come alone?" she asked.

He inclined his head. The hand that rested in his was shaking, but not from fear.

"I have missed you so. I hate this place," she said, vehemently. "It is a prison to me. It eats out my heart, this life. Festini," she said, and again her two hands were laid on his shoulder, and her face searched his, "you cannot understand what an existence this is."

"It is only for a little while, my child," he said.

She was older than he, but his paternal manner was perfect.

"Later we will go away, and leave this dull land for a more pleasant one. Leave these grey skies, for the blue of our Italy, and these drab, drizzling fields for the sun-washed vineyards of our own land."

He kissed her lightly again. He was anxious to get to business. None knew the relations of these two, for Festini kept his secret well. Even in the innermost council of his association, he spoke of her as though she were the veriest stranger.

"I want to go somewhere," she said, moodily, "out of this! I planned to see you in Ireland last year, and at the last moment Ralph would not let me go."

She turned suddenly to him.

"You must have met Marjorie there."

"Marjorie?" he said, innocently.

"We were going together," she went on, "and when I found she had to go alone, after all my planning—"

She shook her head with a sad little smile. "I dared not send a letter by her, or give you an excuse for falling in love with her," she rallied him.

"I don't remember her. What was she like?" said Festini, calmly.

"She remembered you," said Vera. "She maddened me by her chatter of you. I am happy to say that she did not like you very much."

Festini smiled.

"So few people do," he said.

He slipped off his overcoat.

"We are perfectly safe from interruption here?" he asked.

She inclined her head.

"There is no danger whatever."

"Now then," he said, briskly, "let us talk for quite five minutes, dear."

They sat head to head, talking. Five minutes became ten. The young man spoke quickly, vehemently; and she answered in monosyllables. It was nothing to her that he asked so much. She would have sacrificed more than her husband's possessions to please him.

Every law in the world, save the law of gravitation, is suspended in the woman in love. Faith, honour, every known principle went by the board. She had no sense of right or wrong where he was concerned. Only a desire to serve him.

"You had best make the attempt between three and four," he said. "I will be here in the garden, waiting. I have a cycle hidden nearby, and a car will be waiting for me on the London road."

"I wanted to say something to you," she said suddenly. "I hate admitting a failure, and, dearie, I tried so hard."

His quick intuition divined her meaning. "Oh, the money," he said, lightly. "Don't let that bother you. I managed to get some. We've been out of luck lately. This infernal man, Tillizini, has dammed our usual sources. We had a windfall last week, and in a month's time," he said, and she saw the soft light die from the eyes and the delicate mouth harden in one straight line, "in a month's time!" he repeated, "we shall be very rich. And England will be very sore."

With lightning change he brightened again, and was his own insouciant self.

"Don't let the money worry you. We have quite a lot now," he said. "I, somehow, didn't fancy you'd be able to raise the five hundred."

He rose to go and she assisted him with his coat.

"By the way," he said, "that niece of yours, what did you say her name was?"

"Marjorie."

"That is the name," he nodded. "I seem to remember her. Where is she now?" He put the question carelessly.

"She's in the house," replied Vera.

"What a curious coincidence!" he smiled. "She doesn't speak about me nowadays, I suppose?" he asked.

Vera shook her head. It had occurred to the young man that the girl might have referred to their meeting at Victoria.

"Why, of course, how stupid of me!" he said, suddenly. "I saw her the other day, on some station, I remember her now. A tall, healthy-looking, robust person."

His description was not flattering to Marjorie, but it was eminently pleasing to the woman, who was jealous of every other interest he had in life.

"That is not kind," she smiled, "but I think it more or less describes her."

"She was with a tall man, I remember."

"He is in the house too," she said.

He looked at her thoughtfully.

"He is in the house too," he repeated, and his voice was hard.

She thought he was tired, and moved to the window. Her hand was on the curtain. She stood waiting, then, with a little sigh, she nestled close to him.

"I want you so," she breathed. "My God, I do so want you! You don't know what it means, what I feel...."

He laughed, a gentle, tolerant laugh.

He held out his arms, for a second she lay on his breast, her heart beating wildly, perfectly and divinely happy.

"I must go now," he said, gently. "I am afraid of being caught."

With some reluctance she opened the window. He stood for a moment on the balcony, reconnoitring the position.

The coast was clear. In a second he was over the balustrade, and had slipped noiselessly to the ground.

XII — THE SECOND MEDALLION

She waited till he disappeared in the shadow of the garden; then pulled up the ladder and placed it in a drawer within the wardrobe, from whence she had extracted it, and closed the windows.

He had left very definite instructions, and she went over them in her mind to make absolutely sure.

The medallion she knew. She had prepared a drawing especially for this man whose influence was the guiding and dominant thing in her life.

She looked round carefully to remove all trace of the visitor's presence. Then she unlocked the door and went out.

As she passed the little museum, Sir Ralph and his guest emerged. He looked at her in some surprise.

"Hello, Vera," he said pleasantly, for him, "I thought you were with the others."

"I've been doing my accounts," she said, with a little grimace.

Sir Ralph chuckled. In his more pleasant moods he took a humorous view of his own economies.

He was fastening the door of the museum, when Vera intervened.

"I'd like to see those medallions of yours again," she said.

Sir Ralph was pleased. Vera took too little interest in his collection to satisfy him. It was one of his grievances that she did not enter into what he termed the "larger side of his life."

"Come along, come along," he said, "only do not provoke Hilary to a discussion on art, because he is the veriest Philistine."

He chuckled again.

The museum was the one room in the house lighted by electricity. Here once more Sir Ralph had been guilty of an extravagance which was entirely foreign to his nature. He had had a storage battery installed especially for the illumination of his treasure house.

The girl looked at the medallions with more than usual interest. She had seen them before, and recently, though this Sir Ralph did not know. She had a twofold object in asking for this inspection. Her husband had grown nervous as a result of the activity of the "Red Hand," and had signified his intention of changing all the locks. She wanted to make certain that he had not carried out his plans.

Her first glance reassured her. They had not been altered, nor had he changed the position of the medallions.

"They are very beautiful," she said.

In point of fact she thought them very uninteresting, but it was not politic to express this view.

"They grow on you, do they not?" said Sir Ralph, enthusiastically. "I shall make a connoisseur of you in time, Vera."

She went downstairs ahead of the two men, in a thoughtful mood.

It was after midnight when the little party broke up, and retired to their rooms.

Frank was one of the last to go upstairs. He passed through the drawing-room, and found Vera tidying away the chessmen with which Sir Ralph and Hilary had been amusing themselves.

He would have gone straight on, but something induced him to stop.

"Good night, Lady Morte-Mannery," he said.

She was bending over the table and did not trouble to raise her head.

"Good night, Mr. Gallinford," she said.

He still waited.

"I feel that I ought to explain something that is in my mind," he said, a trifle uncomfortably. He had no great command of language, and was somewhat embarrassed.

"I shouldn't, if I were you," she said, quietly. "Let matters go as they are, and be charitable."

She was in a melting mood to-night. For no reason that she could think of, she felt a desire to stand well with the world, and especially with that section of the world which this good-looking English youth represented.

"There is a key-word," she said, "which explains the most contradictory situations, the most unlikely and unthinkable follies. You may know that key-word."

"I only know one," he said, gently, "and that is 'Love.'"

Vera smiled at him. It was a dazzling, human smile, that revealed in a flash the deeps of her nature.

"That is the word," she said, and went on with her tidying.

He stood a second longer; then, with another "Good night" he left her, puzzled and a little ashamed of his own attitude towards her.

At the head of the stairs Marjorie was waiting to say "Goodnight," and in a moment all thought of the woman he had left in the drawing-room below, and her cryptic utterances, were obliterated from his mind.

Vera had been reading before her bedroom fire. She had spent the whole of the night reading and thinking. The reading had been mechanical; she could not recall a single sentence or one situation from the thrilling novel which lay upon her knee.

She looked up at the little clock over the mantelpiece. The hands pointed to a quarter to four.

She rose and took from a hanging cupboard a long dark rain-coat, and this she put on over her dressing-gown, buttoning it carefully so that it should not inconvenience her movements.

She unlocked and opened a drawer of her writing-table and took out a red morocco case.

This she again unlocked with a key attached to a bunch she had taken from under her pillow. The case was apparently empty, but she pressed a spring and the bottom of the box flew up.

Three beautifully fashioned keys lay on the velvet in the false bottom. She took them in her hand, closed the box, and extinguished the light.

She waited by the door for a moment or two, listening. Then she opened it and stepped out into the dark corridor.

She had twenty or thirty yards to walk, but her mocassined feet made no sound upon the thick carpet. The house lay wrapped in slumber, as silent as death.

She could hear nothing save the rattle within the wainscot of a foraging mouse. She walked on until she came to the museum. Here she halted again, listening.

Sir Ralph slept in a room on the farther side and, fortunately, was a heavy sleeper. Hilary had the room on the other.

She inserted the key, opened the rosewood door, took the other key and turned it in the steel door.

Noiselessly the well-oiled lock shot back. She pushed the door open and entered, closing both doors behind her. She could not lock them from the inside, but there was no chance of a casual passer observing that it had been opened, even if casual wanderers were likely at this hour of the morning.

She took from the pocket of her rain-coat a tiny electric lamp, and flashed it over the cases. She found the one she wanted, unshuttered it deftly, opened the glass case, and lifted out the medallion.

She made a quick inspection of it, to make sure that she had the right jewel.

Noiselessly she slipped through the door, locked it behind her, and fastened the outer covering quickly.

Then she turned to retrace her steps to her room.

She took one step and then stopped, rooted to the ground with terror and dismay, for, confronting her, she saw a bulky form.

There was not enough light to show her his face, but she knew it was Hilary George.

"Who's there?" he asked, softly.

She was paralysed with terror. She could not force her tongue to speak.

"Who is that?" he asked, and his voice rose.

With a superhuman effort she recovered her self-possession.

If he spoke louder he would wake Sir Ralph, and that would be the end of things.

"It is I," she said, speaking in the same tone.

"Lady Morte-Mannery? I am sorry," he whispered. "I thought I heard somebody in the grounds, and I listened, but heard nothing more, so I got a little uneasy.

"It's all right," she said, speaking in the same tone as before. "I have been to Sir Ralph's room to get a little veronal. I cannot sleep."

With a whispered apology he went back to his room.

It was on the other side of the treasure house, and she wondered if she had made any noise. Had he seen her come out? His next words lifted a weight from her heart.

"I couldn't see where you came from," he said, "or who you were. I hope I didn't frighten you?"

"Oh, no," she said, lightly.

With another apology he went into his room, and closed the door softly behind him.

She flew along the passage to her room, her heart beating wildly. Once in the room, she locked the door and drew the curtain across it. Then she lit the gas with an unsteady hand. She caught a glimpse of her face in the mirror over the fireplace, and was shocked at its drawn and haggard appearance.

There was still part of the work to be done.

Hilary had heard somebody in the garden. That would be Festini. She looked to make sure that she had the jewel, then she turned out the light again, opened the shutters, and crept out on to the balcony.

She saw a dark figure standing in the shadow of some bushes. The man came forward as she appeared.

"Catch!" she whispered.

He held out his hand as she threw.

He caught the medallion neatly, and put it in his pocket, then turned without a word and plunged into the bushes.

She stood for a moment, a little disappointed feeling in her heart. After all she had risked, all she had dared, she had hoped for some word of thanks.

She was turning to re-enter the room when a sibilant voice held her.

Her heart bounded. He had come back. She looked down at the dark figure beneath. "Did you get it?" he whispered, in a low tone.

"Get it?" she said, in bewilderment, "I have just given it to you."

"Given it to me?" his voice was harsh. "You have given me nothing. I have been waiting here for half an hour."

She staggered back against the balustrade, half sick with fear.

"Tell me, tell me," said the voice impatiently, growing louder. "Who was it you gave it to?"

"I gave it to a man," she said, faintly.

"Which way did he go?"

"Through those bushes," she said. Without another word he ran in the direction the other man had taken.

She had time to get back to the room, close the shutters and pull the curtains, before she fell half-swooning upon the ground.

Festini was light of foot, quick, and with the almost cat-like ability of picking his way in the dark. He had not gone twenty yards before he saw the man ahead.

There was no time for finesse.

Fortunately for him, Festini had changed his plans. He had dropped the idea of coming by cycle, and his car now stood, purring gently, in a little lane which adjoined the house.

As he sighted the man ahead, he whipped out his automatic pistol and fired twice.

Without a sound the man sank to the ground.

Festini had no time to examine his victim. He knew that he was still alive, as he bent over him and searched his waistcoat pockets.

In one of these he had hoped to find the jewel, but it was not there.

But it was in the clasped hand of the stricken man.

Festini found it, wrenched open the fingers, and possessed himself of the prize.

"Now! Do your worst," he hissed, as he swung round and shook his fist, as at a world that was at war with him, "do your worst!"

The sound of the shot had awakened the people of the house. Lights appeared in two or three rooms.

Vera, lying on the floor, was roused to consciousness by a loud knocking at her door.

She got up slowly. Her head was still dizzy, and she staggered as she walked.

"Who is there?" she asked.

"It is I," said her husband's voice. "Open the door. Are you hurt?"

She plunged her hands into a jug of water that stood on the washstand, and passed them over her face. The touch of the chilly water revived her. She dabbed her face with a towel with one hand as she opened the door with the other.

"What is it?" she asked.

She was steadying herself. She had heard the shot, and she was prepared for the worst.

Sir Ralph was in his dressing-gown.

"Where was the firing?" he asked.

"I heard no firing," she said, steadily.

"Somebody fired a pistol in the garden," said Sir Ralph.

She heard Hilary's voice in the passage.

"Are you all right, Lady Morte-Mannery?" said his voice.

"I am quite all right," she replied. "What is wrong?"

Her voice was shaky and high-pitched, but in a dull way she knew that her agitation would be excusable. There had been shots in the garden, somebody had been shot, who? At that moment there came to her a quick pang of fear.

"Somebody is shot?" she asked, tensely. "Who is shot?"

"There was a man in the garden, trying to enter the house," said Hilary's voice. "Possibly he was detected."

Sir Ralph crossed the room, and, opening the shutters, went out on to the balcony. Two men were already on the lawn below.

"Have you found anything?" he called. He was addressing the two hastily-aroused servants who were conducting the search outside.

Vera listened; her heart almost stopped beating, when the groom's voice replied—

"There's a man shot in the shrubbery, Sir Ralph. He looks like a foreigner."

She clenched her hands and waited, rigid , expressionless.

"What sort of man?" asked Sir Ralph, testily. "What do you mean by a foreigner, Philip?"

"Well, he's a clean-shaven gentleman," said the servant. "I don't think he's badly hurt. A tall man."

A great joy surged over the woman.

It was not he; whoever it was, whether this wounded man lived or died, it was not Festini.

She listened. There was a new voice.

"It's all right, Sir Ralph," it said.

She recognized it, and set her teeth. Part of the conversation came to her in little gusts.

"It was just a little clip of a bullet across the temple... that is the second time they have missed me.... I'm afraid you've lost something...."

It was the voice of Tillizini.

In the big hall they assembled, a dishevelled assembly, hastily garmented.

Tillizini's wound was a superficial one. The bullet had struck behind his ear, glancing over the parietal bone and temporarily stunning him. He was very cheerful.

"I only came down to-night by car," he said, "because I received information which led me to believe that the attempt would be made upon you. Now," he said, "I am ready."

He stood up.

"I want to examine your little museum," he said, "and discover what is lost."

"Oh, I couldn't have lost anything from there," said Sir Ralph, confidently. "There are alarms in every window, and almost every pane."

"There are no alarms on the door, are there?" asked Tillizini.

Sir Ralph looked surprised.

"They are not necessary," he said.

He led the way, and the others followed.

He opened the treasure house, and they flocked in behind him. He was a little in advance of Tillizini, and he turned in the doorway to switch on the light.

At that moment Vera saw the evidence of her criminal folly. On the top of one of the shuttered cases was the little jewelled electric lamp which Sir Ralph had in a fit of unusual generosity given her.

Tillizini saw it too. He was as quick as she, and quicker to move. With one step he stood between the tell-tale lamp and the gaze of the half-awake people in the doorway. His hand went out and covered it.

When Sir Ralph turned the lamp had disappeared.

There was a quick inspection.

"It's gone!" cried the knight. "They have taken the Leonardo!"

"I thought they had," said Tillizini calmly, "and I thought I should be able to restore it, but, for the moment, that pleasure is denied me."

"But is it possible?" said Sir Ralph, bewildered. "Nobody could have got in here without my knowing!"

He was almost tearful in his grief.

"It was invaluable," he said. "It cannot be replaced. It is the only one of the kind in the world. What does it mean, what does it mean, Tillizini? You must tell me everything! I insist upon knowing! I won't be kept in the dark!"

He raved and stormed as though Tillizini had been responsible for the theft. It was some time before he became calmer, and then the Italian was by no means informative.

Vera, silent and watchful, waited. Whatever happened, Festini was safe! By now he would be far on his way to London. He had the parcel, that was enough: she had served him, she asked for no more.

From the moment that Tillizini had put out his hand and covered the lamp she knew that he had guessed her secret. Would he betray her? To her surprise and relief he made no reference to what he must have seen and known.

Yet he was distressed and worried, she saw that, but it was with the greater issue, with the danger which confronted civilization.

He walked up and down the hall, a remarkable figure, with the white bandage encircling his head, his hands thrust deep into his pockets, his chin blue and unshaven, his eyes tired, with an infinite weariness.

He took no part in the fruitless discussion as to how the thief effected an entry. He had all the information he required on that subject. He paused in his walk and took from his pocket a shining object, laid it in the palm of his hand and examined it.

Sir Ralph, attracted by the glow of dull gold in his hand, stepped forward with a startled cry.

"Why, that is the locket!" he cried.

Tillizini shook his head.

"It is one very much like it," he said, "but it is not the one. It is the famous locket that was stolen from the Dublin collection, and which is at the present moment supposed to be at the bottom of the North Sea. It was given to a fellow-passenger on that boat to guard and to return to me. You remember I was charged with the investigation of its disappearance?"

He walked to the fireplace.

There were two overhanging gas-brackets which gave a clear light.

He held the medallion with both hands, using only two fingers of each. He gave it a sharp twist and it fell in two.

Sir Ralph uttered an exclamation.

"Why, I did not know that these things opened!" he said wonderingly.

"I could most devoutly wish that they did not," said Tillizini grimly.

He damped his finger a little, and drew forth from the locket's interior what looked like four discs of paper, as indeed they were. They were covered with fine writing, so fine that it was almost impossible to read them without the aid of a reading glass.

"Do you understand Italian?" asked Tillizini.

"A little," said Sir Ralph, "but not enough to read this."

"Take a good look at it," said the other; "it is from the hand of the greatest genius that ever lived since Jerusalem was a vassal state of Rome."

He spoke reverently, almost adoringly, of his famous compatriot.

"That is the hand of Leonardo da Vinci," he said in a hushed voice.

"And what is it all about?" asked Frank, "and isn't it written backwards?"

He had been examining the microscopic writing with his keen eyes.

Tillizini smiled.

"The master wrote with his left hand invariably, always working back to the left. This will help you."

He drew from his pocket a tiny mirror in a leather case.

"Read," said Tillizini.

Frank carried the little discs nearer to the light, and brought them with the mirror closer to his eyes. Marjorie, watching him, saw his lips move as he read the Italian, saw his brows pucker in a puzzled frown, then her lover looked up suddenly.

"Why," he said, "this is all about a plague." Tillizini nodded.

"The Great Plague," he said, "or, as modern scientists call it, the Fourth Plague, which broke out simultaneously in Italy and Ireland in the same year. It was the one plague which our modern doctors are unable to understand or fathom. As a matter of fact, the only man who understood it was Leonardo da Vinci. He was, as you know well, Sir Ralph, more than a painter. He had the scientific mind perfectly developed. He was the first to foresee the coming of the aeroplane and the armoured ship. He was an engineer, a sculptor, a chemist, and—"

He spread out his hands.

"What is the use? I cannot enumerate his qualities," he said. "He was so above the heads of his contemporaries that they were unable to realize what kind of genius was in their midst. Even posterity can hardly do him justice. He alone understood the Fourth Plague, its meaning and its cause.

"That plague came into existence by the cultivation of a germ, though this, of course, he did not know because the microscope was denied him, but he guessed it, with that wonderful, God-like intuition of his, he guessed it," said Tillizini, his face glowing with enthusiasm and pride.

"The conditions under which the plague came into being, conditions which were undreamed of, even by those who saw them under their eyes, were revealed to Leonardo da Vinci. Ordinarily," he went on, "they would in this year of grace be produced."

"What do you mean by that?" asked Sir Ralph.

"Under the modern system," said Tillizini, "that plague could never appear again. But there are six drugs which you might find in the British Pharmacopoeia," he continued, "which, if you were to mix them, would produce a gas."

He spoke impressively, and with the assurance of the practical scientist.

"That gas, passed through a filter of vegetable matter, would set up conditions which made the plague of 1500 possible."

"Good God!" said Frank. "Do you mean to say that you can produce a plague synthetically?"

Tillizini nodded.

"That is exactly what Leonardo da Vinci discovered. This is the secret."

He held the flimsy discs in his hands.

"There is no doubt that Leonardo did produce a plague synthetically, two years after. At any rate, some such outbreak occurred in the town where his laboratory was situated. It is believed that, as a result of that plague, Mona Lisa Gioconda lost her life."

"Oh, that is the woman in the picture," said Marjorie.

"That is the woman in the picture," repeated Tillizini, "the one woman in the world whom Leonardo ever loved. The one great softening influence that ever came into his life. His investigations into the cause of the plague he set forth, concisely, on these little filaments. The lockets he fashioned himself. One, as you know—"

"I know the history," said Sir Ralph. "I was telling Mr. Gallinford only the other day. How extraordinary it is that that old-world story should be revived."

"But why do the 'Red Hand' want these lockets?"

"They only want one. Either one will do," said Tillizini. "Don't you realize? To-morrow, with the aid of a man with even the most elementary knowledge of chemistry, they could devastate London, and not only London, but the whole of England, or, if it please them, the whole of Europe, working from different centres."

As the little party stood stricken to silence, the full horror of the danger dawning upon them, Tillizini heard a long-drawn sigh.

Vera had stumbled forward in a dead faint, and Frank had just time to catch her before she fell.

XIII — THE ABDUCTION OF MARJORIE

It was a week after the burglary at Highlawns that a perfectly happy man went whistling to his work. He walked with a brisk step, carrying his lunch in a gaily-coloured handkerchief, with a tin can full of tea for his breakfast. George Mansingham raised his eyes to the sky, which was just turning grey, in thankfulness at his freedom.

Work had been found for him through the medium of Hilary George, at a little farm outside the town. He and his wife had been installed in a tiny cottage on Sir Ralph's estate. To give Sir Ralph his due, he had freely admitted the injustice of the sentence he had passed; if not to the man, at least to himself, which was something; and it needed little pleading on the part of Hilary George, who had taken an interest in the case, to induce him to let his untenanted cottage to the man he had wronged.

Early as the hour was, he found his employer and his son up and about. There is much work to be done before the sun comes up over the edge of the world. There are horses to be fed and groomed, sheep and cattle that require attention, cows to be milked, and milk to be carried.

The sky grew lighter, the sun came up, it seemed to him with a rush, but he was too busy to notice the progress of the time. At half-past eight nature called him to breakfast. He sat down to his frugal meal, first placing two nosebags on the heads of the horses, for he was now engaged in ploughing the ten-acre lot Farmer Wensell farmed. His meal quickly disposed of, he pulled a bulky book from the inside of his jacket pocket and began to read. He had a passion for self-education, and at the moment Merejowski's Forerunner, which Marjorie had lent him, had a special significance, not only for him, but for the whole of England. He was so intent upon the pages of this wonderful romance that he did not notice the girl who was crossing the field with such free strides.

He heard his name called and looked up; then he sprang to his feet, hat in hand.

"You're very absorbed, Mansingham," smiled Marjorie.

"Yes, miss," said the other, "it's a wonderful book, and he's a wonderful man. I'm not surprised all the world's talking about him just now."

"It's not because of his genius that they are speaking of him," said the girl, gravely.

She carried a paper under her arm; in fact she had been down to Burboro' Station to get the journal.

"It's a terrible business, miss," said the man. He put the book down. "It doesn't seem possible, in a civilized age, and in a country like England. Is there any fresh news this morning, miss?"

She nodded gravely.

"The 'Red Hand' have addressed the Premier," she said, "and they have demanded ten million pounds, an act of indemnity passed by the House of Commons, and freedom to leave the country."

The man looked incredulous.

"Why, they'll never get that, will they, miss?" he asked. "It's against all reason, a demand like that! Suppose it's not true, suppose they haven't discovered this plague—"

She shook her head.

"There's no doubt about it, Mansingham," she said. "Mr. Gallinford knows it to be true. He has been investigating, looking up old documents relating to the plague of 1500. These men have it in their power to decimate the whole of England."

The subject they were discussing filled the minds of men throughout Great Britain that day; nay, throughout Europe. Wherever civilized people foregathered, the cable and the telegraph had carried the news of the threat which overhung the country. It was the final demand of the "Red Hand," a demand which at first had been pooh-poohed, and had been discussed by Government officials as a problem which called for immediate solution.

The "Red Hand" had acted swiftly. Three days after the locket had disappeared from Burboro' a startling proclamation of the "Red Hand," printed in blood-red characters, had covered the hoardings and the walls of London. Then it was for the first time that England woke to a realization of the terrible danger which threatened her. It was incomprehensible, unbelievable. It was almost fantastic. Men who read it smiled helplessly as though they were reading something which was beyond their understanding. And yet the proclamation was clear enough. It ran:

To the People of London.

We, the Directors of the "Red Hand," demand of the English Government

(a) The sum of Ten Million Pounds.

(b) An act of indemnity releasing every member of the Fraternity from all and every penalty to which he may be liable as a result of his past actions.

(c) A safe conduct to each and every Member of the "Red Hand," and facilities, if so required, for leaving the country.

In the event of the Government's refusing, after ten days' grace, we, the Directors of the "Red Hand," will spread in London the Plague which was known as the Fourth Plague, and which destroyed six hundred thousand people in the year 1500. The bacillus of that plague is in our possession and has been synthetically prepared and tested.

Citizens! Bring pressure on your Government to accede to our demands, and save us the necessity for inflicting this terrible disease upon you!

It bore no signature or seal. It was absurd, of course. Evening papers, necessarily hurried and having little time to analyse its true meaning, made fun of it. But a different note appeared in the comments of the morning papers. Every known scientist and doctor of note who was reachable had been interviewed, and they one and all agreed that there was more than an idle threat in the pronouncement.

The papers called it variously, "The Terror," "The Threat of the 'Red Hand,' "Blackmailing London," and their columns were filled with every available piece of data concerning the terrible scourge which had swept through Italy and Ireland in the year of desolation.

"It's a terrible business," said Mansingham again. "I am afraid there is something in it."

The girl nodded.

With a courtesy which is not usually found in men of his class, he accompanied her to the end of the field, and assisted her across the rough stile leading on to the road. She had made a detour from the little station to speak to Mansingham. She was interested in him, and it was a pact between the barrister and herself that she should keep, as he put it, a friendly eye upon his protégé.

It was a glorious morning; the world was flooded with the lemon sunlight of early spring. The trees were bright with vivid green, and primroses and wild violets flowered profusely by the hedgerows. She shook away the gloom and depression to which the thought of this terrible menace had subjected her, and stepped out briskly, humming a little tune.

Half-way across the field, Mansingham, retracing his steps, picked up one of the papers she had been carrying, and hurried after her.

She had a twenty minutes' walk before she reached Highlawns, which stood some quarter of a mile from the town's limits, but she was of an age, and it was such a morning, when one's feet seem to move without effort, and song comes unbidden to the lips.

She heard the whirl of a motor-car behind her, and moved closer to the hedge to allow it to pass. Unconsciously she turned to see who was the occupant. At that moment the car jarred itself to a standstill at her side. A young man, dressed from head to foot in a white linen dust-coat, sprang out.

"Count Festini!" she cried in amazement.

"Count Festini," he repeated, with his most charming smile. "I wanted to see you, won't you get in? I am going up to the house?" he said.

She hesitated. She would much rather have walked that morning. But it would have been an act of rudeness to have refused his offer of a lift, and besides, it occurred to her that she was already overdue for breakfast, and Sir Ralph's temper of late had not been of the best.

She stepped into the car, and at that moment Mansingham, a little out of breath, broke through the hedge behind it.

"What a curious idea," Marjorie said, as Festini took his place beside her.

"What is a curious idea?" he asked.

"A closed car on a day like this," she said. "Why, I thought you Italians loved the sun."

"We love the sun," he said, "untempered by such winds as you seem to produce exclusively in England."

He stepped forward and pulled down a red blind which hid the chauffeur and the road ahead from view. She watched him without understanding the necessity for his act. Then with a quick move he pulled the blinds down on each side of the car. It was now moving forward at a great pace. At this rate, she felt, they must be very near indeed to Highlawns. They had, in fact, passed the house, as the embarrassed Mansingham, clinging to the back of the car and waiting for it to slow up so that he could restore the girl's paper, saw to his bewilderment.

"Why do you do that?" the girl asked coldly. "If you please, Count Festini, let those blinds up."

"In a little while," he said.

"I insist," she stamped her foot. "You have no right to do such a thing."

She was hot and angry in a moment as the full realization of his offence came to her.

"In a moment," he repeated; "for the present we will have the blinds down, if you don't mind."

She stared at him in amazement.

"Are you mad?" she asked, angrily.

"You look very pretty when you're angry," he smiled.

The insolent assurance in his tone made her feel a sudden giddiness. They must have passed Highlawns by now.

"Stop the car," she demanded.

"The car will stop later," he said; "in the meantime," he caught her hand as she attempted to release the blind, "in the meantime," he repeated, holding her wrist tightly, "you will be pleased to consider yourself my prisoner."

"Your prisoner!" exclaimed the affrighted girl. Her face had gone very white.

"My prisoner," said Festini, pleasantly. "I am particularly desirous of holding you to ransom. Don't you realize," his eyes were blazing with excitement, "don't you realize," he cried, "what you are to me? I do. In these last few days," he went on, speaking rapidly, "I have seen all the wealth that any man could desire. And it is nothing to me. Do you know why? Because there is one thing in the world that I want more than anything, and you are that thing."

Both his hands were holding her now. She could not move.. She was as much fascinated by his deadly earnestness as paralysed by the grip on her arms.

"I desire you," he said. His voice dropped until it thrilled. "You, more than anything in the world, Marjorie. You are unattainable one way; I must secure you in another."

The girl shrank back into a corner of the car, watching the man, fascinated. She tried to scream, but no sound came. Festini watched her, his eyes glowing with the fire of his passion. His hot hand was closed over hers almost convulsively.

"Do you know what I'm doing!" he said, speaking rapidly, "do you know what I'm risking for you? Can't you realize that I am imparting a new danger to myself and to my organization by this act? But I want you; I want you more than anything in the world," he said passionately.

She found her voice.

"You are mad," she said, "you are wickedly mad."

He nodded.

"What you say is true," he answered moodily, "yet in my madness I am obeying the same laws which govern humanity. Something here," he struck his breast, "tells me that you are the one woman for me. That is an instinct which I obey. Is it mad? Then we are all mad; all animated creation is mad."

The fierce joy of possession overcame him; she struggled and screamed, but the whir of the engine drowned her voice. In a moment she was in his arms, held tightly to him, his hot lips against her cheeks. He must have caught a glimpse of the loathing and horror in her face, for of a sudden he released her, and she shrank back, pale and shaking.

"I'm sorry," he said, huskily, "you, you say I am mad, you make me mad."

His moods changed as swiftly as the April sky. Now he was pleading; all the arguments he could muster he advanced. He was almost cheerful, he swore he would release her, reached out his hand to signal the driver, and repented his generosity.

Then he spoke quickly and savagely of the fate which would be hers if she resisted him. It was the memory of that tall, handsome lover of hers that roused him to this fury. He was as exhausted as she when the car turned from the main road, as she judged by the jolting of the wheels. After ten minutes' run, it slowed down and finally stopped.

He jumped up, opened the carriage door and sprang out, then turned to assist her. A cold, sweet wind greeted her, a wind charged with the scent of brine. She stood upon a rolling down, within a hundred yards the sea stretched greyly to the horizon. There was no house in sight save one small cottage. About the cottage stood two or three men. She uttered a cry of thankfulness and started off towards them, when a laugh from Festini stopped her.

"I'll introduce you myself," he said sarcastically.

She turned to run towards the sea, but in two strides he was up to her and had caught her by the arm. Then a huge hand gripped his neck, with a quick jerk he was spun round. His eyes blazing with anger, he turned upon his assailant. George Mansingham, tall and broad, grimed with the dust of the road, for he had maintained an uncomfortable position hanging on to the back of the car for two hours, met the vicious charge of Festini with one long, swinging blow, and the Italian went down to the ground stunned.

The girl was dazed by the suddenness of the rescue, until Mansingham aroused her to action.

"This way, miss!" he said.

He caught her unceremoniously round the waist, swung her up as if she were a child, and leapt across a ditch which drained this section of the downs.

"Run!" he whispered. He too had seen the men and guessed they were in the confederacy. The girl gathered up all her reserve of strength and ran like the wind, Mansingham loping easily at her side.

The wind carried the voices of their pursuers. One staccato shot rang out, a bullet whistled past them, then some one in authority must have given the order to stop firing. And indeed it was more dangerous for the men than for the fugitives.

There was a coastguard station half a mile along the cliff road, and, although neither the girl nor Mansingham realized the fact, they instinctively felt that the coastline offered the best means of escape. Then suddenly Marjorie tripped and fell. Mansingham stopped in his stride and turned to lift her. As he raised her to her feet he uttered an exclamation of despair.

Facing him were two men, indubitably Italians, and their revolvers covered him. He had come against the "Red Hand" outpost.

It was all over in ten minutes. The pursuers came up, the girl was snatched from his protecting arms. He fought well; man after man fell before his huge fists. Then a knife, deftly thrown, struck him by the haft full between the eyes and he went down like a log.

Festini, breathless, his face marred by an ugly redness which was fast developing into a bruise, directed operations.

"If you make a sound," he said, "or attempt to attract the attention of any person you see, you will have that person's death on your hands, and probably your own."

He spoke curtly, impersonally, as though she herself were Mansingham.

"Do not hurt him," she gasped. She referred to the prostrate form of the farm-labourer, now stirring to life. Festini made no answer. He was of a race which did not readily forgive a blow.

"Take her away," he said.

He remained behind with his two familiars. "I think we will cut his throat, Signor," said Il Bue, "and that will be an end to him."

"And an end to us," said Festini; "this coast is patrolled, the man will be found, and the whole coastline searched."

He walked a dozen paces to the edge of the cliff and looked down. There was a sheer fall here of two hundred feet, and the tide was in.

"There is twenty feet of water here," he said, significantly.

They carried the reviving man by the head and feet to the edge of the cliff. They swung him twice and then released their hold, his arms and legs outstretched like a starfish. Round and round he twirled in that brief space of time, Festini and the other watching. Then the water splashed whitely and the dark figure disappeared.

They waited a little while, there was no reappearance, and Festini and his lieutenant retraced their footsteps to the cottage, the third man following.

The period of ultimatum was drawing to a close. For four days longer England had the opportunity of agreeing to the terms which the "Red Hand" had laid down.

In his big library at Downing Street, occupying the chair which great and famous men had occupied for the past century, the Prime Minister, grave and preoccupied, sat in conference with Tillizini.

The Italian was unusually spick and span that morning. He had dressed himself with great care, an ominous sign for the organization he had set himself to exterminate. For this was one of his eccentricities, and it had passed into a legend among the criminal classes in Italy, that a neat Tillizini was a dangerous Tillizini. There is a saying in Florence, "Tillizini has a new coat, who is for the galleys?"

The Prime Minister was fingering his pen absently, making impossible little sketches upon his blotting pad.

"Then you associate the disappearance of Miss Marjorie Meagh with the operations of the 'Red Hand'?"

"I do," said the other.

"And what of the man, Mansingham?"

" That, too," said Tillizini. "They were seen together in a field where Mansingham was working, his book and his coat were found as he had left them, and then he and she walked together to the stile. He is seen by another labourer to walk back slowly across the field, to suddenly stoop and pick up something, probably the lady's handkerchief or bag, it is immaterial which. He runs back to the stile, jumps over, and evidently follows the lady. From that moment neither he nor she are seen again. One woman I questioned at a cottage by the roadside remembers a big car passing about that time. I place the three circumstances together."

"But surely," said the Prime Minister, "they would hardly take the man. What object had they? What object in taking the lady so far as that was concerned?" Tillizini looked out of the window. From where he sat he commanded a view of Green Park, a bright and spirited scene. The guard had just been relieved at the Horse Guards, and they were riding across the parade ground, their cuirasses glittering in the sun, their polished helmets so many mirrors reflecting the rays of light. He watched them sadly, and the great crowd that marched on either side of them. Not all the arms of England, all her military and naval strength, her laws and splendid institutions, could save her from the malignity of the "Red Hand."

He turned with a start to the Prime Minister, and found that gentleman regarding him curiously.

"In a sense," he said, "I do not mind this abduction, always providing that neither of these people are injured. I cannot understand why they should have bothered; but it is these side issues of private vengeance which invariably bring the big organizations to grief."

"Seriously, Professor Tillizini," said the Premier, "do you think that these men will carry their threat into execution?"

"Seriously, I do," said Tillizini. "Your experts scoffed at the idea of the 'Red Hand' being able to cultivate this particular germ. The 'Red Hand's' reply must have been a little startling to them." He smiled. "If I remember rightly they sent a little of the culture to your Bacteriological Institute. Animals which were inoculated died with all the symptoms which have been described by the fifteenth-century writers."

The Premier nodded his head.

"We cannot give the money, that is impossible; you recognize that, Professor?" Tillizini assented.

"It would mean the negation of all law; it would create a precedent which would put an end to all the authority of civilization; it were better that all England should be ravaged by this disease than that a single penny should leave the Treasury. That is my view. I am prepared," he said quietly, "to accept not only the responsibility of that action, but the first consequence of these men's machinations. This I have intimated through the public press. The only hope is that we may secure the culture, and not only secure it, but locate the laboratory where the cultivation is being made. It is a hope," he shrugged his shoulders. "I know you are doing all you can, Tillizini," he said quickly, "and Scotland Yard—"

"Scotland Yard is working splendidly," said Tillizini. "Your police organization is rather wonderful."

He rose to his feet.

"Four days," he said, "is a very long time." "You will take any steps you deem necessary for the public safety?"

"You may be sure of that, sir," said Tillizini.

The Premier twisted his blotter in his preoccupation.

"They say of you, Professor," he said deliberately, "that you do not hesitate to commit what in the eyes of the law-abiding world might be considered as criminal acts, in order to further justice."

"I have never hesitated," said Tillizini, "if you mean—"

"I mean nothing in particular," said the Premier; "only I tell you this, if you deem it necessary to go outside the law to administer preventive punishment, I assure you that I will secure you the necessary indemnity from Parliament."

Tillizini bowed.

"I have to thank your Excellency for that," he said, "and you may be sure I shall not abuse the power, and that no crime I commit will ever need an act of indemnity."

The Premier looked up in astonishment.

"Why?"

"Because," said Tillizini, with his sweetest smile, "my crimes are never brought home to me."

With another bow he left the room.

Outside the house in Downing Street. Inspector Crocks was waiting.

"I got you some telegrams," he said, genially. "I am rapidly deteriorating into a private secretary'."

Tillizini smiled. A feeling of affection had grown up between these two men, so differently constituted, so temperamentally apart. When Crocks had been detailed to assist Tillizini in his work, there were many sceptical people who smiled behind their hands, for anybody more unlike the detective of fiction than the inspector could not easily be imagined. Yet he was a shrewd, clever man, subtle to a point of brilliancy. A rapid and effective organizer, with a knowledge of the criminal underworld which few men possess.

Tillizini tore open the telegrams; he read them twice, then he crumpled them into a ball and thrust them into his coat pocket. The letters, after glancing at the address and the postmark, he placed unopened in the inside pocket of his frock coat.

"I didn't show you the telegrams," he said to the other, "because they were in code."

In a few words he communicated the gist of their contents. Tillizini's code-book was in his head.

"I am going to see my decoy now."

"Is he still alive?" asked the inspector with simulated surprise.

"He was, a few minutes ago," said Tillizini. For once he did not treat the subject facetiously, and the inspector knew that the question he had put in good-humour had a serious application.

"I secured him a position," said Tillizini suddenly; "he is an outside porter at Victoria, It will afford him an excellent opportunity of becoming acquainted with contrary humanity."

"And at the same time he will be able to give you a little information," said Crocks. "I think it is an excellent scheme. He doesn't look clever, and I don't think he is particularly clever, but he has got the power which so few police officers possess, unfortunately. The moment a man begins to look important his value decreases."

Tillizini laughed.

"Oh, unimportant man!" he said cryptically.

A few minutes later the two parted. The detective went back to Scotland Yard and Tillizini hailed a cab and drove to an address in South London.

At half-past twelve that day the fast train from Burboro' to Victoria steamed slowly into the big terminus. Vera Morte-Mannery was one of the first to descend. Her foot touched the platform almost before the train stopped.

She walked quickly through the barrier into the large space at the end of the station.

She looked round anxiously, and then up at the clock. The man she sought was not there. She strolled aimlessly from one side of the station to the other, and was returning to the bookstall, when Festini, with rapid strides, came into the station.

She caught his eye and he checked himself and turned about carelessly. He walked out of the station and she followed. At his uplifted finger a car came out of the rank and drew alongside the pavement.

Without a word she got in and he followed. They drove in silence until the car turned into Hyde Park and slowed down in obedience to the regulations.

Then she turned to him suddenly and, with a breaking voice, asked—

"Where is Marjorie Meagh?"

He raised his eyebrows.

"Marjorie Meagh?" he asked. "You do not mean to tell me that you have brought me to London to ask me a question like that?"

" Where is Marjorie Meagh?" she asked again.

"How on earth should I know?"

"Festini," she said, pleadingly, "let us be frank with one another. Marjorie has been taken by the 'Red Hand.' You are the 'Red Hand.'"

"Hush!" he muttered, savagely; "don't shout, people could hear you on the sidewalks!"

His manner to her had changed. It was a little cold, a little impatient, more than a little intolerant. She had detected the changed atmosphere the moment she had met him.

She pressed her lips tightly together and remained silent for a little while.

"What is your object in taking her?" she asked.

"That is hidden from you. Do you not trust me?"

"Trust you!" she laughed bitterly. "Have I not trusted you to the fullest extent?" she asked. "That question should rather come from me. You do not trust me, Festini."

It was less a statement than a pleading. She wanted him to deny it, but no denial came.

"There are things which it is not right for me to tell you."

"Why?" she asked; "is there any secret of the 'Red Hand' which I do not know?"

He smiled a little uneasily.

"You did not know anything about the Fourth Plague," he said, softly.

"I do not complain of that," she said, "it was too great a thing to trust with any man or woman. But there is nothing so subtle in this kidnapping of Marjorie Meagh."

He spread out his hands with a gesture of helplessness.

"I cannot tell you," he said. "There is something behind this which you cannot know."

"There is something behind it which I can guess!" she said fiercely. "You love Marjorie, you have taken her because you love her. Don't deny it. I can see it in your face. Oh, you liar! You liar!"

He had never seen her like this. It was a new force he was encountering, one which at once pleased and piqued him.

She had been all softness, all yielding to him before, an easy conquest for this handsome man, with his soft voice and his eloquent eyes.

In her anger she was a little terrible, but she did not terrify him. He was used to opposition, and had a quick way with it. There was enough of woman in him to appreciate her feelings. But, like the autocrat he was, he resented her revolt, and in his resentment said more than it was wise, under the circumstances, to say.

"Yes, it is true," he said, coolly. "I do love her. Why should I deny it? I do not love you any less because I love her. She is on a different plane to you and I."

Vera was breathing quickly; her bosom rose and fell with the intensity of her pent up rage. She did not speak again for a minute; she was conquering an insane desire to throw herself from the car, to run anywhere out of his sight, as she had gone, she knew, out of his heart. The fires of humiliation and jealousy burnt too fiercely within her for words.

Again and again she checked the wild torrent of speech that rose to her lips and choked in the checking.

And this was the end! The end of her dream, the reward for all her work, for all her treachery to those who loved her, the last stretch of the happy road which she had fondly thought led to eternity.

From time to time he looked at her out of the corner of his eye.

"I understand," she said at last, speaking composedly, "your great plan has come to fruition. You have no further use for me?"

"Do not say that, Vera," he said.

He was immensely relieved to discover how well she had taken the news, which, cold-blooded as he was, he had no desire, and if the truth be told, no intention of telling her.

"You are indispensable," he said. He tried to take her hand, but she withdrew it. "It is only the exigencies of the scheme we have in hand which has prevented me from taking you more fully into my confidence. As to Marjorie, I want you to be generous," he said. "I want you to realize—"

"Oh, I understand," she said, wearily. "Were you ever sincere, Festini, were you ever faithful?"

She looked at him searchingly.

"I swear," he began.

"Don't swear," she said. "I think I understand." She smiled bravely. "I'll get out here," she said. "I'd like a little walk. This was not exactly the outcome of the morning's meeting that I expected," she went on; "although I was jealous, I never realized that my suspicions were true."

He tried by argument to persuade her to remain with him, but she was determined. She tapped the window and the car drew up. As she alighted, he assisted her. She held out her hand.

"Good-bye, Festini," she said. His eyes narrowed.

"You must see me again, there is no goodbye with me," he said, abruptly. "I have told you you are indispensable, I mean that."

She made no reply. Gently she relaxed her clasp, and her hand fell listlessly to her side. Then she turned abruptly and walked away.

He stood watching her until she was out of sight. Could he trust her? He had a large knowledge of men, a larger of women. He had weighed all the chances; she would not betray him, he thought. These English people love to suffer in silence, to hug to their secret hearts their greatest griefs.

He smiled, shrugged his shoulders, and, turning to the driver, directed him to a fashionable restaurant. For men, even great conspirators, must lunch.

He stopped the car in Oxford Street to buy an evening newspaper. It was filled, as had been the morning journals, with speculations on the Fourth Plague. Would the "Red Hand" put their threat into execution? One journal had found a scientist who had discovered a specific, another gave a perfect pen picture of Tillizini. Wild and improbable rumours found prominence, there was nothing of any real account. He was closing the paper when a little paragraph which had evidently been inserted to fill up caught his eye at the bottom of the column.

"The unfortunate man, Mansingham, who has added to the tragic variety of his career by being associated with the disappearance of Miss Marjorie Meagh, was an expert swimmer, and at the annual meeting of the Burboro' Aquatic Club last night sympathetic references were made to his disappearance."

Festini frowned. A swimmer? Of course it was absurd. But there might have been grave danger in throwing him into the water. He was stunned, though, and three days had passed without any sign of his reappearance.

He knew, by careful inquiry, that nobody had been picked up on the coast, but it sometimes happened that weeks elapsed before the sea gave up its dead. It was absurd to bother about that.

But throughout his luncheon he found the thought intruding in his mind. Suppose this man turned up? It would have been better to have followed out the suggestion of Il Bue and have killed him right away.

The waiter brought him his bill, and he paid, tipping the servant lavishly.

He walked out of the hall into the big vestibule of the restaurant, selected a cigar at the little cigar counter, and strolled out into Piccadilly.

His car, driven by a trusted member of the "Red Hand," followed him along the broad, crowded thoroughfare at a snail's pace.

At the corner of Piccadilly Circus he suddenly came face to face with Frank Gallinford.

The Englishman was looking ill; the strain of the past few days was telling on him. The loss of his fiancée was preying on his mind; he had not slept. His agents were searching the country from end to end. He had also established a little police organization of his own, for Frank Gallinford was a fairly wealthy man.

The two men stopped, staring at each other for the fraction of a second, then Festini held out his hand with a suave smile.

"How do you do Mr. Gallinford?" he said.

Frank was in no mood for conversation or condolence. He uttered a few conventional words, shook hands hurriedly and passed on, leaving Festini to finish his stroll.

Frank had not gone twenty yards before somebody pressed his arm softly. He looked round. A tall man was standing at his side. At first he did not recognize him in his rough workman's kit and his little moustache, but when he spoke he knew him.

"Go back after Festini," said Tillizini quickly. "Talk to him about anything you like, hold him in conversation for a few minutes," he turned and walked back with the other a little way, "and when you get into St. James' Street turn off to the right. The street is up. Induce him by any art in your power to go to the other end of that street."

"But why?"

"No, do not ask, 'Why,'" said Tillizini. He gave one of his rare gestures of impatience. "Do as I tell you."

Frank nodded. Though he had no heart for the job, he quickened his steps and overtook Festini.

Tillizini watched them. He saw them strolling aimlessly along, and turn into the street he had indicated. The waiting car on the other side of the road entered the street and then stopped; the road was up, and beyond half-way down there was no thoroughfare. The chauffeur looked round anxiously. He had to back out and make a detour by the way of the lower end of Regent Street and Piccadilly. He had another alternative, which was to wait. He looked undecided. He was assisted in his decision as to what he should do by the gesture of a policeman, who ordered him back to the main street.

Very slowly the car backed out. It was a minute or two before he could bring the long Napier into the stream of traffic moving up towards Piccadilly Circus. There was a block here, and another wait ensued.

Tillizini had posted himself where he could watch every movement. He saw the look of anxiety on the chauffeur's face. The opportunity he had been waiting for for the last two hours now presented itself. He threaded his way through the block of traffic and passed the car. He took something from his pocket and, bending over the rear wheel, pressed down his hand upon it. A broad strip of rubber with a steel clamp at either end.

Deftly he fixed it over the wheel. In its centre an arrow head projected. It had been carefully prepared and only the expert, interested in the accessories of cars, would have thought it unusual.

With one glance to see that his work had been well done, he slipped through the traffic, and gained the other side of the road. He walked a little way down Regent Street, from thence he saw the two men talking. Festini was walking back. He had missed the car and had understood why it had failed to follow him.

Tillizini saw him take a hurried farewell of Frank and walk quickly up the street. The professor smiled. It appealed to him, this spectacle of Festini and his car playing hide-and-seek with one another.

He did not attempt to rejoin Frank, instead he called a cab, which came reluctantly, for this man in working clothes did not inspire confidence, and drove straight to Scotland Yard.

That night every police station in England received a notification, and in the early hours of the morning, policemen on foot, cyclists and mounted men were searching the wet roads for the track of a motor car which displayed an arrow at regular intervals.

XV — THE HOUSE BY THE RIVER

From her window Marjorie could see the broad and sluggish river. When the fog did not veil every object from sight, she caught a glimpse of big ships passing up and down; fussy little tugs drawing strings of lighters, brown-sailed barges that went with stately leisure to the sea. In the foreground was marshland, uncultivated.

The sluggish river, for such it was at a distance of a quarter of a mile, was the River Thames; the marshland was that unlovely stretch of swamp on its north bank, between Southend and Barking.

By putting her face close to the window she could see a small, low-roofed building, tarred and weatherproof, from which men in white overalls came and went.

The house she was in was an old one, as houses go. It was built of brick; the rooms were lofty and cold and a little damp.

Even in the room which had been allotted to her use, the paper had peeled off the wall in great pieces, and not even the fire, which the hard-faced Italian woman who attended her kept fed, dispelled the chilly dreariness of the apartment.

She had been brought here by night from the house on the cliff. She had lain down to sleep after supper in her Kentish prison and had awakened to find herself lying in the room she now tenanted.

The knowledge that they must have drugged her food filled her with panic.

The day following her arrival she had refused to eat or drink, and now it was not until the Italian woman had partaken from the dishes she supplied, before Marjorie's eyes, that the girl consented to touch the food.

Fortunately, she numbered amongst her accomplishments a working knowledge of Italian. Of late she had polished up her acquaintance with the language. Frank's work mainly lay in Italy, and she had seen the necessity for becoming proficient.

But she received no satisfactory reply to any of her inquiries. She had not seen Festini since that day on the cliff, though she had heard his voice often enough.

She guessed rather than knew that in the little low-roofed house near by, was being prepared that terrible culture which was to bring England to her knees in submission.

Everything that Festini could do to relieve the monotony of her life, he had done.

She was plentifully supplied with books and papers, and to serve her table he had secured a perfect Italian cook.

The only man she had spoken to was a tall giant of a man, whom she had seen on the cliff with Festini.

He answered her questions gruffly, and in monosyllables.

He had merely come into the room, she gathered, to see to the security of the bars which had been fixed outside the window. She was ill with anxiety; she dare not give her imagination its rein.

It was Frank she thought of, Frank, whom she knew would be distracted with grief; and at night she alternately wept and prayed for the strength and sanctuary of his arms.

It was on the third day following her abduction. She was sitting trying to read by the window, when the click of the lock brought her to her feet.

She heard the voice of Festini outside, and in a moment he had come into the room, locking the door behind him.

They stood confronting one another. She had walked swiftly to the centre of the room, and placed the table between them.

"Well?" he said, with his pleasant smile, "I hope you have everything you want."

She made no reply at once. Then—

"I want my freedom," she said.

"That," he said, with a little bow, "I am sorry I cannot grant you. It is necessary for my health and security that you should stay a little longer. Afterwards, I hope to make you the wife of one of the richest men in Europe."

"That will never be," she said, steadily. "I would sooner be the first victim of the plague you threaten, than endure that humiliation."

He winced at the words.

"It is no humiliation," he said, a little haughtily. "In my veins runs the best blood of Italy. It is an honour to be the chosen bride of Festini."

She was amazed at the unexpected vanity of the man.

She had never regarded him, even at the most friendly period of their relationship, as more than a rather good-looking, well-mannered member of the middle classes. That he should esteem his birth as being sufficient to make him superior to censure was a strange point of view.

She looked at him, in spite of herself, with an added interest.

"I ask you to be my wife," he said.

He emphasized the words.

"You ought to realize that, in addition to doing you an honour, I am also acting with great magnanimity. You are here alone," he said, "entirely and absolutely at my mercy. You are surrounded by men and women who would question no act of mine, however barbarous it might seem to you. Do you understand?"

She understood too well.

She was safe unless she made quasi-friendly relationships impossible. She had need to temporize.

He may have guessed what was passing in her mind.

"Understand," he said, "there is no escape from here, except as my wife. I will be patient without you. I have been patient with you," he went on. "To-morrow a priest will marry us according to the rights of my Church."

"To-morrow!" she gasped.

"To-morrow," he said, a little mockingly. "It is rather soon, is it not? And you have no trousseau!"

He waved the objection away.

"That is a detail which can either be arranged or can be overridden."

He made no attempt to touch her.

"May I sit down?" he asked.

She nodded, and he drew a chair forward to the table and seated himself.

"I think I ought to take you a little into my confidence," he said, in his pleasant, matter-of-fact manner. "It is necessary to expedite matters. Your friend, how do you pronounce his name, Mansingham? was picked up by a fishing smack. I think he swam out to sea and picked up the smack, but it is immaterial. He is alive, and, I have reason to believe, talkative."

He saw the look of hope spring up in her face, and smiled.

"The fact that he will be able to identify me with this act of abduction," he went on, "embarrasses me, but, fortunately, our scheme is so far advanced that there is no longer any necessity for me to disguise my association with the 'Red Hand.'"

"The only thing which is a trifle annoying is that I must stay in this deadly place a few more days. All the work that is to be done my agents can do. But for your presence here it would be an impossible situation. Not for all the gold in England could I rusticate by the banks of the Thames, alone."

His dazzling smile bewildered the girl. He had a trick of discussing the most outrageous propositions with a serious and convincing air. It was all superficial, but then his superficiality bit deeper into him than into most men.

At heart she knew him to be a cold-blooded and remorseless man, who would stop at nothing to gain his ends. It was only that the veneer of civilization was thicker, that the brute within him did not lie so close to the surface, which distinguished him from his comrades.

But the streak of cruelty was there, as he showed.

"By the way," he said, "I met Mr. Gallinford the other day, and condoled with him upon your disappearance."

"You brute!" she flamed. "How dare you mock me!"

"I like you when you are like that," he said, admiringly. "You almost tempt me to continue to tell how ill and worn he looks."

He laughed, but there was no note of merriment in the sound.

"A singularly thick-headed man! Had he been an Italian he would have known by my face, by the change in my eyes when your name was mentioned, that it was I" he pointed to himself, "who had robbed him. But then these Englishmen are so phlegmatic! They soon forget. You must not worry very much about your Frank," he said, as he rose to go. "In a year or two he will have married some comfortable Englishwoman, and have settled down to a life made up with shooting pheasants and discussing defective drainage."

She was incapable of reply.

He went out of the room and locked the door behind him, leaving her alone, with her head on her arms, weeping from very anger.

He found Il Bue in the room below with two men who had just come in from the laboratory he had arranged in the wooden shed.

"Well?" he asked, moodily, as he flung himself into a chair at the head of the table. "What are the developments?"

"Signor," said one of the men, "everything is ready. We have secured perfect cultures, even more perfect than those dispatched to the Bacteriological Institution." Festini nodded.

"To-morrow I shall receive the Government's reply. I have asked them to advertise that reply in the columns of a newspaper."

"And what will it be?" asked Il Bue, his eyes fixed upon Festini's face.

Festini shrugged.

"Who knows?" he said. "I think at the eleventh hour they will agree to my terms."

One of the assistants in white was a thick-set man with a sour, bad-tempered face. He took no part in the subsequent discussion on the methods to be adopted for the distribution of the plague.

Festini had made elaborate precautions and had issued exhaustive literature for distribution amongst the members of the "Red Hand."

He was sincere in his desire that the agents of his organization should escape the consequences of their own villainy.

When the discussion was finished, the surly man jerked his head round to Festini. He was sitting on his right hand, his elbows on the table, his big, fleshy hands clasped.

"What about this woman, Signor Festini?" he asked.

The young man looked at him steadily.

"' This woman '?" he repeated, softly, "I do not know who you mean."

The stout man jerked his head upwards. He was the kind of man who moved in jerks.

"She who is upstairs," he said.

Festini got up very slowly from the table.

"You will understand, Gregorio," he said, in his honeyed tones, "that you will never refer to that lady in such a way. Indeed," he said, carefully, "you will never refer to her at all."

"There are no secrets from the brethren," grumbled the man. "We all want to know what is the plan with regard to her." Without a word Festini's hand leapt out; his quick, strong fingers caught the other by the throat; with a sidelong twist he forced the man's head back over the table.

Festini was a strong man despite his frail physique.

"You dog!" he hissed in the man's purple face. "Must I answer to you for all I do?" The man struggled to recover his balance, but a long bright blade flashed in front of his eyes.

Festini hesitated, then he released his grip, and the man staggered up to his feet.

"Remember this," said the Count. "Remember it all your life, Gregorio. It may serve you well one day, the recollection." The man was livid and shaking.

"I'm sorry, Signor," he said, humbly; "it was thoughtless. I did not intend to offend your Excellency."

With a curt nod Festini dismissed him.

"And understand," he said, "that I will not spare any man who speaks slightingly or lightly of the lady who is to be the Countess Festini. There is my plan, if you wish to know it. That is enough, too much, perhaps, certainly enough. I give you my best , you must give me obedience and faith. That is all I ask."

He was in no mood of tolerance.

George Mansingham had arrived in England, and by this time Tillizini knew what he had already guessed. London was unsafe for Festini, and he was the type of man who scorned any disguise.

He must fret away his time in this God-forsaken spot; the fulfilment of his plans demanded it.

He stopped in the house long enough to don the white overall which had distinguished his companions, and went into the long wooden shed, Il Bue and the two men joining him at the entrance of the hut.

The only light came through a big skylight. House and shed had formed part of a boat-builder's establishment, long since bankrupt and fallen into decay. It suited his purpose admirably. It was far enough away from the high road to obtain seclusion. He had a plausible excuse for the presence of his men. The premises were ostensibly part of the properties of a little company he had formed some time before for the manufacture of synthetic rubber.

There is something about synthetic rubber and its manufacturers and inventors which keep an amused public at bay.

The shed was divided into two parts. In the first there were a number of test tubes, retorts and scientific apparatus upon a large bench.

The entrance to the second room was obtained through a stout door, which was fastened by two padlocks.

These the big man unfastened. Before he opened the door he pulled up from his chin an antiseptic mask, which he brought over his face and secured to the hood of his white gown.

The others followed his example.

They took up rubber gloves from the bench in the outer room and drew them on. Il Bue pulled the door open and a faint sweet scent came out to greet them.

In the centre of the inner and smaller compartment was a long narrow table on which, at intervals, rested four deep porcelain dishes under glass bell-covers.

They were no more to the sight than narrow strips of glass coated with a light-brown gelatinous substance, but each glass case held death in a terrible form.

Festini looked at them curiously. It was almost impossible to believe that these innocent-looking strips of dull glass could play so powerful a part.

"That is all?" said he, half to himself.

"That is all, Signor," said Il Bue.

His big face was twisted in a puzzled grin.

"It seems a very simple thing," he said, suspiciously; "why, I could smash it out of existence with a blow of my fist."

The man with the sour face looked up at him sideways.

"You would die very soon," he said.

He was the chemist of the party, a brilliant man with strange gifts, who had been brought into association with the "Red Hand" and found an outlet in their operations for the lawless and perverse spirit within him.

Festini turned and led the way from the room. He waited till Il Bue re-padlocked the door, then he stepped out of the shed, slipping down his mask.

The fresh air came to him like a sweet, refreshing draught; it seemed to him that he had tasted the very atmosphere of death and desolation in that tiny room; that it was already tainted with the plague he was about to spread wide-cast.

He made no other attempt to see the girl; he was satisfied with that one interview. He remained in his room, reading by the aid of a portable electric lamp such comments of the Press upon the "Red Hand" as his agents had collected.

At ten o'clock there were two new arrivals. In one of these Festini was particularly interested; it was the priest he had secured for the marriage ceremony.

Psychologists have endeavoured to get at the state of Festini's mind; to analyse by set formula the exact proportions. Was he wholly villain? Were the fantastic acts of chivalry, preposterous as they were, remembering the circumstances in which they were displayed, indications of a better nature?

Tillizini, in his exhaustive analysis of the man's character, had attributed such acts as this contemplated marriage as merely evidence of habit. Festini's long association with men and women of his class had endowed him with an habitual respect for certain conventions. This was Tillizini's estimate, and was probably an accurate one, for he knew the man.

The priest he had chosen had been brought post-haste from Italy, and had travelled night and day. He was a man known to the association as being "safe": he himself was suspected of complicity in certain outrages which had shocked Italy in the year before the great trial. He himself had stood with the other sixty prisoners in a cage in the criminal court, but, thanks to ingenious perjury, he had escaped punishment.

Festini greeted him without cordiality, with the grave respect which a true son of the Church shows to his spiritual superior, and with the faint hint of patronage which the greater intellect instinctively adopts towards the lesser.

He gave orders for the priest's accommodation, and, after the brief interview, was again left alone.

It was near midnight when Festini threw himself down on a truckle bed to snatch a few hours' sleep. In the early horns of the morning his spies would bring him news of the Premier's reply. He fell into an uneasy, fitful sleep, a sleep disturbed by bad dreams, such as were not usual with him.

There came a light knock and he went to the door. Il Bue was waiting.

"What is it?" asked Festini.

"One of the brethren has just come in," said the man, who was palpably disturbed. "He came on his cycle from where he has been watching the London road, and he says that some soldiers are marching from London."

Festini made a gesture of impatience.

"Did you wake me to tell me that?" he asked, irritably. "Haven't you been long enough in England, my friend, to know that soldiers have nothing whatever to do with police work? This is not Italy, it is England. Go, tell your scout to return to his post, to watch not for the army, but for Tillizini and his friends."

He went back to his room and again lay on the bed, pulling a soft, camel-hair rug over him. He tossed from side to side but could not sleep; he got up after a little while, and went out. A man was keeping guard outside the door.

"Go to Catrina," he said, "and tell her to make me some chocolate."

A few minutes later the woman brought him in a steaming bowl on a tray. She set it before him and he acknowledged it with a curt word of thanks, when a thought occurred to him.

"Catrina," he said, calling her back, "your lady is well?"

"Yes, padrone," she replied. "I saw her two hours ago, before she was asleep."

Festini nodded.

"See her again now," he said, "I will go up with you."

Taking a lamp from the bracket in the narrow passage of the house, the woman led the way upstairs, and Festini followed.

He waited outside the door whilst the woman unlocked it and entered. He heard a smothered exclamation.

"Padrone!" cried the woman, wildly. "Padrone!"

He rushed into the room. The little bed in the corner was empty. The window was open and three of the bars were missing. Marjorie Meagh had gone!

XVI — TILLIZINI ADDRESSES THE HOUSE

Though it was past midnight the streets of London were alive with people; shops were open, lights blazed from windows which ordinarily would have been in darkness. The motor services which carried the Londoner to and from his home were still running; special editions of the evening papers were on sale in the streets, and about the House of Commons, where the crowd grew in intensity, they found a ready sale.

Between Whitehall and Victoria Street some thirty thousand people had assembled, but the police had no difficulty in controlling the assembly or in securing a passage way for the constant stream of cars which were passing to and from the House of Commons. The character of the crowd was an interesting one. These were no idle sightseers, attracted by the chance of a little excitement; it was the silk-hatted middle class of England, overcoated, muffled, bespectacled, waiting patiently for news which meant all the difference between life and death to them.

For once in its history the House of Commons was sitting in secret session. At eleven o'clock that night, by the Speaker's direction, the galleries had been cleared, and strangers had been excluded, not only from the lobby, but from the precincts of the House. Parliament had resolved itself into a National Jury.

At five minutes after twelve a great car, covered with dust, came slowly along Whitehall. It bore three small lamps on its radiator, arranged in the form of a triangle. Unchallenged the car passed Bridge Street and into Palace Yard. About the entrance of the House were a crowd of policemen, but they made a way for the tall man in the dusty coat who sprang from the seat by the side of the driver. Two men were waiting for him; Hilary George, M.P., was one, and Inspector Crocks the other.

The three passed into the interior of the House and made their way to a small Committee room which had been prepared for them.

"Well?" asked Crocks. His face was of an unusual pallor, and he spoke with the irritability which is peculiar to the man undergoing a great nervous strain.

Tillizini slowly divested himself of his great coat, laid it across a chair, and walked to the fire. He stood for a while, warming his hands at the blaze; then he spoke.

"I have located them," he said, "definitely."

"Thank God!" said Crocks.

"There is no doubt?" asked Hilary. Tillizini shook his head. He took a book from his inside pocket, opened it, and extracted three slips of paper. They were advertisements cut from a newspaper of the week before.

"I don't know," he said, "whether you have noticed these?"

They bent over the table, the three heads together, reading the advertisement.

"I cannot understand it," said Hilary; "this is an advertisement offering good prices for pigeons." He examined the other. "This is the same," he said.

"They're all the same," said Tillizini, quietly. "Do you notice that they advertise that they want old pigeons?"

Hilary nodded.

"The address is at a place in London. The man who advertised had thousands of replies, and has made thousands of purchases, too. Throughout the week basket after basket of birds has come consigned to him at the various London termini; they have been collected by the agents of the 'Red Hand' and forwarded to Festini."

"But why?" asked Crocks, puzzled. "He's not going to start a pigeon-shooting competition?"

Tillizini laughed. He had walked back to the fire and was bending over it, his hands almost touching the flames.

"If you will believe me," he said, "I have been looking for that advertisement for quite a long time." He straightened himself and stood with his back to the fire, his hands behind him. Then he asked suddenly: "How is the 'Red Hand' to distribute the germs of this plague? Has that thought ever occurred to you? How can they, without danger to themselves, spread broadcast the seeds of the Black Death?"

"Good Heavens!" said Hilary, as the significance of the move suddenly dawned upon him.

"To-morrow morning," Tillizini went on, "if the Premier's reply is unfavourable, they will release these thousands of pigeons, and release also, in a portable form, sufficient of the culture to spread death in whichever neighbourhood the pigeon lands. Naturally, being old birds, they will fly straight back to the homes they have left. It is very ingenious. They might of course have done the same thing by post, but there was a certain amount of risk attached to that. The present method is one which would appeal to Festini. I arrested a man this afternoon who has been collecting the birds. He is obviously one of the 'Red Hand,' though he protests against such an imputation."

"What is to be done?" asked Hilary. "You had better see the Prime Minister at once."

The door opened and a young man came in hurriedly.

"Is Professor Tillizini here?" he asked.

Hilary indicated the detective.

"Will you come at once, Professor? The Prime Minister wishes you to stand at the bar of the House to explain to the honourable members exactly the position."

Tillizini nodded.

He followed his conductor along the broad corridor, across the lobby, through two swing doors. He suddenly found himself in a large chamber; it gave him the impression of being dimly lighted. On either side he saw row after row of faces rising in tiers. At the further end, behind a big table surmounted by a gold mace, sat a wigged and gowned figure on a canopied chair. Near the table on his left a man rose and spoke to the Speaker. Tillizini could not hear the words he said. The moment afterwards the grave figure in the wig and gown invited him forward.

Tillizini knew something of the august character of this legislative assembly; he knew, since it was his business to know, with what jealousy it guarded its doors against the unelected stranger, and he experienced a feeling of unreality as he walked along the floor of the House and made his way, at the invitation of the Premier's beckoning finger, to a place on the Front Bench.

The House was in silence. A faint murmur of "Hear, Hear," had greeted him, but that had died away. A strange figure he made, still powdered with the fine dust of the road, unshaven, grimy.

He sank down on the cushioned bench by the Premier's side, and looked with curious eyes at the Mother of Parliaments.

Amidst dead silence the Prime Minister rose and addressed the Speaker.

"Mr. Speaker," he said, "it is within my province, had I so desired, to have asked you to vacate the chair and for the House to resolve itself into a Committee. Under those circumstances we should have had extensive powers, one such power being our right to summon any stranger before us to give evidence.

"But the time is so very short, and the issues are so very serious, that I have asked you to rule, as an extraordinary ruling, that Professor Tillizini be allowed to address the House from this place."

The Prime Minister sat down, and the bearded man in the chair looked at Tillizini, and nodded again. For a moment the professor did not understand its significance; then a whispered word from the Premier at his side brought him to his feet, a little embarrassed, a little bewildered.

He spoke hesitatingly, halting now and then for a word, thanking the House for its indulgence and for the remarkable privilege it had granted him.

"The Prime Minister," he went on, "has asked me to give you a brief outline of the history of the 'Red Hand.' He thinks, and I agree, that you should be made fully aware of one fact only that the 'Red Hand' threatens to perform."

For five minutes he traced the history of the organization; its growth from the famous Three Finger Society of Sicily; he spoke briefly of its crimes, both on the Continent and in America, for he had the details at his finger-tips, and he himself had been engaged in unravelling many of the mysteries which had surrounded the work of these men.

"I do not know," he said, "what plans this Parliament has formed for ridding the country of so dangerous and so terrible a force. No plan," he spoke earnestly and emphatically, and punctuated his speech with characteristic gestures, "which you may decide upon, can be effective unless it includes some system of physical extermination. I do not make myself clear, perhaps," he said, hurriedly, "although I have a very large acquaintance with your language." He emphasized his point with one finger on the palm of his hand. "These men are going to destroy you and your kind. Believe me, they will have no compunction; the plague will be spread throughout England unless you take the most drastic steps within the next few hours. There is no existing law on the statute books which exactly provides for the present situation. You must create a new method to deal with a new crime, and, Mr. Speaker, whatever this House does, whatever steps it takes, however dreadful may be the form of punishment which it, in its wisdom, may devise, it cannot be too drastic or too severe to deal with the type of criminal organization which the 'Red Hand' represents. I can, if I wish," he said, with a smile, "arrest fifty members of the 'Red Hand' to-night. I could, with a little care, succeed in assassinating Festini."

He spoke in a matter-of-fact tone, as though assassination were everyday work, and a little shiver ran through the House. He was sensible to such undefinable impressions in others.

"You do not like the word?" he said, with a smile, "and neither do I. I used it because I felt that it was a word which would be more in keeping with the facts from your point of view. To me, some removals are justified; they are more, they are necessary. One must meet cunning with cunning, crime with crime. The law does not adequately meet all modern crime, even the English law. Science has produced a new type of criminal; but the modern parliaments of the world have not as yet devised a new type of punishment. The criminal code requires drastic revisions, as drastic as those which it received when it erased from its statute book such awful and vindictive punishments as were accorded to sheep-stealers."

He went on to tell as much of his later discoveries as he felt it was expedient to announce to the House. He could never overcome his suspicion of crowds. The House of Commons, with its serried ranks of members, was a crowd to him, an intellectual, a sympathetic and brilliant crowd, but a crowd nevertheless, which might contain, for aught he knew, one man who would betray his plans to the enemy.

The House gasped when told the story of the pigeons.

"I understand," he said, "that you have an Act in contemplation; the terms of that Act have been briefly communicated to me, and I can tell you, Mr. Speaker, and the members of this House, that there is no provision in that measure which is not justified by the circumstances. Within seven days," he said, solemnly, "this country will be ravaged by the most malignant form of epidemic disease that has been known in modern history. The horrors of the great plague of London will be multiplied, the ports of every foreign country will be closed to your commerce; you will be shunned by every grain-bearing ship that sails the sea.

"You are face to face, not only with death in its most terrible form, but with starvation, with anarchy, with civil war perhaps. And yet, knowing this, I tell you that you would be false to your great traditions if you paid one single penny to this infamous confederacy."

He sat down amidst a murmured cheer.

In a few minutes he had walked out behind the Speaker's chair, and was in the Prime Minister's sitting-room. That statesman came in soon afterwards.

"The Act will pass to-night," he said; "the Lords are sitting, and I hope to get the Assent early in the morning. Can you rest to-night, Professor?"

Tillizini shook his head.

"There is no rest for me to-night," he said.

He looked at his watch. The hands pointed a quarter after twelve. An attendant brought in a tray with coffee. After he had retired, the Prime Minister asked—

"You are satisfied with such steps as we have taken?"

Tillizini nodded.

"Yes, I think the number will be sufficient."

"We have sent four infantry brigades by route march to-night," said the Premier. "The cavalry and artillery are coming from Colchester."

"The destroyers?" asked Tillizini.

"They left Chatham at sunset to-night with orders to steam slowly up the river." Tillizini nodded again.

"There will be one waiting for you at Tilbury," said the Prime Minister, "that was in accordance with your wishes."

A few minutes later Tillizini entered his car, wrapped in his great coat, and the great Mercedes sped noiselessly out through the guarded gate, through the press of people in Whitehall, into Trafalgar Square, then turned to the right along the Strand. It slowed down to pass a market van, which had emerged from the street leading from Waterloo Bridge. As it did so a man walked quickly from the sidewalk and leapt on to the footboard of the car.

He was a middle-aged man, poorly dressed, and he was apparently Italian, for it was in that language he said—

"Signor Tillizini?"

"Yes," said Tillizini, in the same language.

The man made no reply. His hand went up with a lightning jerk. Before his fingers had closed on the trigger, Tillizini's had grasped the pistol near the trigger guard, He half rose to his feet and, with a quick swing of his body such as wrestlers employ, he pulled the man into the car. It was all over in a second. Before the passers-by and the loungers about the sidewalk realized what had happened, the man was in the car, his pistol reposed in Tillizini's pocket, and the Italian detective's foot was pressing lightly but suggestively on his throat.

"Keep very still," said Tillizini, bending over. "Put your hands up, so."

The man obeyed with a whimper of pain; then something hard and cold snapped around his wrists.

"Now you may sit up," said Tillizini.

He dragged the man to his feet and threw him into a corner seat. From his breast pocket he produced a little electric lamp and flashed it in the man's face.

"Oh, yes," said Tillizini, with a little laugh. "I think I have seen you before."

He recognized him as one of the many thousands of agents which the "Red Hand" possessed.

"What are you going to do with me, Signor?" asked the man sullenly.

"That I will tell you later," replied the other.

In the East India Dock Road he stopped the car at a police-station and bundled the captive out. The inspector was inclined to resent the spectacle of a strange-looking foreign gentleman hauling a handcuffed compatriot into the charge-room. But at a word from Tillizini he became obsequiousness itself.

"Search him," said Tillizini.

He unlocked the handcuffs, a pair of his own, and two constables, with scientific deftness born of experience, made a quick but careful examination of the man's possessions. He seemed to be well supplied with money, Tillizini noticed; he had no papers of any kind. A pencil and two stamps and some unaddressed telegraph forms, comprised the sum of his property.

Tillizini carried the telegraph forms to the inspector's desk and examined them carefully. They were innocent of address or writing, but he saw impressions which showed that another telegram had been written on top of one of them with pencil. He looked at it closely but he could detect nothing. From his pocket he took a soft crayon and gently rubbed the impression over. Gradually the words came to light. The address was unintelligible. It had evidently been written upon a harder substance. There were two words in Italian, and Tillizini had little difficulty in deciphering them.

"Lisa goes," he read.

He looked at the man.

"Who is Lisa?" he asked. But before the prisoner could shake his head in pretended ignorance, Tillizini knew, and smothered an exclamation that came to his lips.

Vera had gone to her sometime lover. Here was a complication indeed.

XVII — MARJORIE CROSSES THE MARSH

Marjorie had retired for the night at eleven o'clock. She had given up an attempt to bar the door against intruders, for her efforts to barricade herself in had been resented by the woman, and, moreover, they had been so ineffectual as to render the attempt a waste of time and energy.

The house boasted one storey, the ground and the first floor; her room was on the upper floor at the back of the house. It had been chosen partly for the reason that it was undoubtedly the most habitable of the apartments which the ramshackle dwelling boasted, and partly because from this position she could see little or nothing of the movements of those members of the "Red Hand" who were engaged in the nefarious work of preparing the culture.

The night was an unusually clear one, and when, after half an hour of sleeplessness, she arose to escape from the tumult of thought which assailed her, her steps turned instinctively to the one outlet upon the world which the room afforded. She leant her arms on the old-fashioned window-sill and looked wistfully out to the twinkling points of light upon the river.

No sound broke the stillness of the night, the house was wrapped in silence. Now and then there came to her the faint echo of a siren farther down the river. She stood for some time, and then, with a shiver, realized that the night was by no means warm.

Festini and his servants had provided her with a long black cloak. She took it down from its peg on the wall and wrapped it about her. Her fingers were still busy with the fastening at her throat, when a little sharp, metallic tap at the window made her turn with a start.

Her heart beat quickly as she stood motionless, watching. She waited nearly a minute before it came again. It was as though somebody were at the window.... There could be nobody there, she told herself. She walked softly to the window and opened it. The bars had been so placed that they came almost flush with the brickwork. It was impossible for her to see who stood directly below.

She waited a little while longer and heard a hiss. She stood back. She did not know why, but it seemed that the unknown was warning her. Then something fell on the floor at her feet.

She stooped and ran her hand lightly along the uncarpeted boards. Presently she found what she sought. It was a little pebble, but she was led to it by catching her fingers in a thin piece of twine, and by and by she had drawn up to the window a piece of thicker string.

She understood its meaning now. Rapidly she drew it in. There was a heavier weight at the end of it, and presently she came upon a stout, closely-woven hemp rope. This was the end of the series. Somebody on the ground without held the rope with gentle firmness.

Her hands trembling with excitement, she knotted the end about one of the bars of the window, and felt the man outside test the strength of it. Again and again he pulled as she watched anxiously the amateur knots she had tied.

To her delight they showed no signs of slipping.

The rope went taut again. There was a steady strain on it. She heard no sound, and it was with a startling suddenness that the bare head of a man appeared above the window-sill; he reached up and clasped a bar and came to rest sitting lightly on the ledge without.

"Don't make a sound," he whispered. He went to work methodically. The bars had been screwed on to a square of wood fitted into the window space, stapled and morticed into the brickwork itself.

She could not see his face, and he spoke too low for her ordinarily to recognize his voice; but this was Tillizini, and she knew it. He lost no time. A little electric lamp showed him the method by which the bars were fastened. They had been screwed on from the outside, sufficient security for the girl within, though offering no serious obstacle to a man armed with a screwdriver without.

Tillizini worked at fever heat. Clinging on to one bar, with one of his thin legs thrust through into the room, he had two bars out in ten minutes.

As he removed them he handed them to the girl, and she placed them quietly upon the bed.

He stepped lightly into the room, re-tied the rope to one of the remaining bars, fastened one end about her waist, and assisted her through the window.

"Stay at the bottom until I come," he said.

She had not long to wait; whilst her fingers were still unfastening the knot around her waist Tillizini was coming down the rope hand over hand.

"Wait!" he whispered. He disappeared into the darkness in the direction of the shed. Piled up alongside was basket after basket of a pattern. He walked swiftly along, unfastening the trap-fronts as he did so. Soon it would be light, and at the first sign of dawn the pigeons would begin their homeward flight. He returned to the girl.

"Move very slowly," he whispered, "and follow me."

They crouched down, and almost at a crawl crossed the big yard, the limits of which were still defined. They gained the marsh which lay between them and the river.

Still Tillizini showed no signs of abandoning his caution, and the girl, cramped and aching from her unaccustomed exertions, wondered why he still moved almost on hands and knees when the danger seemed to be past.

The ground underfoot was swampy, with every step she went ankle deep into liquid mud, she was breathing with difficulty, and her back ached with an intolerable, nagging pain. She felt she could go no farther; it seemed to her that she had been moving for horns across miles of country, although, in fact, she had not gone two hundred yards from the house, when Tillizini stopped, and motioned her forward.

"Stay here," he whispered.

Although the marsh was apparently a dead level, there were little hummocks and rises at irregular intervals, and toward one of the former he moved stealthily.

She thought she saw the black figure of a man sitting on the one dry space in the marsh, but fancy plays strange tricks on a dark and starless night, and her heart had beaten wildly a dozen times during that agonizing crawl at imaginary figures contesting her way of escape.

The man on the hummock was no figment of imagination, however; he sat cross-legged like a tailor, a big sheep-skin rug about his shoulders, a long-barrelled revolver on his knee.

The duty of outpost in this direction had fallen to Gregorio, the sour-faced man who had aroused Festini's anger earlier during the day.

The "Red Hand" had established a system of sentries to preclude any surprises, and from where he sat Gregorio could keep a clear lookout upon the river approaches to the house.

He sat wide awake and alert, his fingers touching the trigger of his revolver. All this Tillizini guessed rather than saw. He knew that any act of violence, unless it was unexpected and deadly, would produce an alarm. The bold way was the only means possible. He rose and straightened himself, and went squelching forward across the oozy ground.

Gregorio heard him and sprang to his feet.

"Who's there?" he asked, softly.

"It is I, Brother," said Tillizini in Italian.

He yawned.

"Is anything wrong?" asked Gregorio, peering forward in the darkness to distinguish the newcomer.

Tillizini's answer was to yawn again loudly and prodigiously, as one who had been recently wakened from his proper sleep and had reluctantly obeyed the summons.

His yawn extended for the half a dozen paces that separated him from the sentry.

Gregorio had no suspicion. His finger mechanically went from the trigger to the butt of the revolver, which now hung loosely at his side.

"What d—?" he began again.

Then like a bolt from a crossbow Tillizini launched himself at the man's throat. His left hand gripped the revolver, he wrenched it from the man's hand. In that motion he had him by the throat, and the two men were rolling on the ground.

The sentry's yell for help was strangled in his throat.

Marjorie, a dozen yards away, kneeling in the cold marsh with clasped hands and parted lips, heard the sound of the struggle and heard, too, a stifled cry, and then a silence.

A few seconds later Tillizini came back to her.

"You may get up," he said softly, "there is no need for any further concealment."

He gave her his arm and assisted the half-fainting girl the remainder of the journey.

At the water's edge he found the little Canadian canoe that had carried him across the river, and helped her into it. He followed, and, seizing his paddle, with two strokes he sent the little craft swiftly into the stream.

XVIII — THE WOMAN

Festini stared dumbfounded at the window. He saw the dangling rope, and knew in what deadly peril he stood.

The girl had been rescued from the outside; he saw the bars laid on the bed, and the little heap of twine and cord beneath the window told its own story.

With a curse of rage he ran from the room.

In a moment he had the house roused.

In the rooms below a dozen trusted members of the "Red Hand" were sleeping; another dozen were out watching the roads.

"They cannot have gone far," said Festini. "On your life see that they are captured."

He himself went with a man in the direction of the river, the most likely way of escape. He knew every position his scouts occupied, and he half walked and half ran through the clogging marsh to where Gregorio had been posted. He was the most reliable of all the men who were on duty.

He came to the foot of the little hummock, and called softly.

Gregorio made no reply.

Festini ran up the gentle slope. He flashed his lamp over a prostrate form.

"Turn him over," he said calmly.

He looked down at the dead man's face, and a weary foreboding of defeat oppressed him. Without a word he turned and walked slowly back to the house.

Every step he took said, "Tillizini! Tillizini! Tillizini!"

This was the end. He knew it. His mind was less occupied with thoughts of escape than with a riot of plans to make his exit memorable.

The Premier had refused.

He did not require the arrival of a messenger to tell him that. Tillizini had located the laboratory, that fact was evident. How, Festini could not guess, but the last card of the "Red Hand" was not played. He had still the germs of this terrible disease. They themselves would be the first victims and leave behind their dreadful heritage to humanity.

He wondered why the professor had not struck at him. Surely at this, the eleventh hour, he felt no compunction? Festini dismissed the possibility with a smile. He knew the breed too well to imagine that pity or any tender sentiment could influence the anthropologist.

Then he remembered the girl. She explained all. It would be Tillizini's first care to place her in safety.

He left word that the guard should be narrowed to a smaller circle about the house. He went to his room, searched his pockets and found letters which he had no desire should fall into the hands of the enemy. He burnt them, and sat down to the table to write a letter. He was in the midst of this when Il Bue came in.

"Our men have found a woman," he said.

"A woman!" Festini jumped to his feet, his eyes kindling.

"It is not your lady, Signor," said the man, and the other's heart sank like a plummet.

"Where did you find her? What was she doing?"

"Making her way to the house," said Il Bue.

"Bring her here."

In a few minutes the man returned and ushered a woman into the room.

Festini, dapper and handsome in his well-fitting greatcoat, his feet covered with the mud of the marsh, stood, his hand resting on the bare table, an electric reading-lamp the only illumination the room possessed.

It was innocent of furniture; save for the dull glow of the fire in the broken hearth, it was cheerless. The damp had stripped the walls of its paper, there was an indefinable air of decay in the room.

The woman standing in the doorway took all this in as she advanced slowly towards him, her eyes fixed on his face.

"Vera!" he gasped, and stared.

She nodded.

"Let your man go away," she said.

At a sign from Festini the big man withdrew, closing the door behind him.

"Why have you come? How did you get here? How did you know I was here?" He fired the questions at her.

She made no reply, taking off her long fur coat deliberately.

"I have come," she said at last, "to be with you at the great moment."

His brows knit. "What do you mean?" he said.

"You are doomed, Festini. I discovered it last night. Sir Ralph had confidential information from the Government, ordering him to be present at the end."

"'The end '?" he repeated. "I don't understand. When is the end to be?"

"To-day," she answered steadily.

"But you, you," he said, "why have you come?"

She did not speak for a moment, her eyes were still fixed on his.

"I have served you well," she said slowly, "let me serve you to the end."

"But there may be danger for you."

"There will be danger," she said.

"I cannot allow this; go back to your friends. Leave me to fight this out alone."

She shook her head with a little smile.

"We fight this out together, Festini. I have come to stay. They have traced you."

"Tillizini?" he asked, without resentment. She nodded.

"He saw your car in town, suspected you, fastened a band to the wheel. That band bore a particular mark. I did not know this until last night. The police all over the country have been examining the roads for signs of that car. Tillizini did the rest."

"I see. What is happening?"

"The place is surrounded," she said.

"Surrounded?" he did not raise his voice. He was not, apparently, alarmed. He put the question eagerly; it seemed to her that his interest in the method which had been employed to trap him was greater than any dread of the consequence.

"How do you mean?"

She led him to the window of the room. It was on the opposite side of the house to that which Marjorie had been confined, and commanded an uninterrupted view of the country for six or seven miles. The overnight mists had cleared away and it was a calm, still night. The low hills of the horizon could be easily distinguished.

He saw a sprinkling of lights that were familiar to him. They were the lights of a hamlet, two miles distant, and at intervals a flickering gleam told him where the road lay.

They watched in silence. Then, of a sudden, they saw a new light. It was whiter than the others; it flickered three times, and was dark. Flickered again with irregular intervals, and kept winking and winking, as though it were a candle blown by the wind.

"I understand," he said, "that is a signal lamp. Are there soldiers?"

She nodded.

"There are a dozen regiments on this side alone," she said.

"Infantry?" he asked.

"Yes," she replied, "and horse soldiers, and I saw guns coming through Witham."

"And on the river side?" he asked.

"I think they have some torpedo boats. They came up from Chatham last night."

He walked round to the other side of the house, but could see nothing. He went back to his room and found a pair of night glasses, and searched the river with a long and steady scrutiny.

Then he distinguished the low-lying hulls of the destroyers, anchored in midstream, their lights out, no sign of life.

He nodded slowly.

"I understand," he said, for the second time. "Come back with me."

He put his hand on her shoulder affectionately, and she thrilled at the touch.

She had not asked about Marjorie, but now the thought occurred to her. He divined it before she spoke.

"The girl is gone," he said. "Tillizini released her less than half an hour ago; he also released some pigeons," he said, with a quiet smile.

He told her what had happened.

"I think it is best," she said, gravely.

There was no resentment in her heart against his treachery, nor did he feel it necessary to explain his act, or express his contrition.

Those two had much in common, as he had always realized. They took things for granted.

"I suppose," he said, after he had sat at the table, his head in his hands, deep in thought, "there is no question of surrender?"

She shook her head.

"They will accept no surrender," she said. "They have come to exterminate you. They dare not take you for fear of your disseminating the plague."

"They are very wise," he said; "but yet I think...."

He bit his knuckles thoughtfully.

"Perhaps," he began again, then shrugged his shoulders.

He walked with a firm step to the door and called in Il Bue. In a few words he made the position clear.

"Get the rifles out of the cellar," he said, "and serve out ammunition to the men. We are going to make a fight for it, but I tell you there is no chance of escape. The least we can do is to leave behind a little souvenir of our earnestness and bona fides."

When the man had gone, he turned to Vera. "Dear," he said, gently, "you must go back."

"I have come to stay," she said. "I want no better end than this."

He looked at her thoughtfully, tenderly. Then he took her face in both his hands, and kissed her on the lips.

"As you will," he said; "it will strengthen me as nothing else could strengthen me, to have you by me."

He kissed her again, and her head fell on his shoulder, her arms stole about his neck.

She was happy. Whatever other joys life had held for her, they were as nothing to this.

An hour before dawn Festini left the woman who had braved so much for him, and went the rounds. A new sentry had been posted in the place of Gregorio. Festini was returning and crossing the room which had served as a common room and office for the band, when the tinkle of a bell held him. He turned back.

He had had the house connected by telephone, but an hour before the arrival of Tillizini, though he did not know this, the wires had been cut. He walked to the instrument and took down the receiver. Was it possible that by some chance they had overlooked the wire, and that he could communicate with the agents of the "Red Hand" in London? The thought had not occurred to him before, but at the first word which reached him his lips curled in an ironic smile.

"Is that you, Festini?" said the voice.

"Yes," replied the Count, "my friend Tillizini, I think?"

"It is I," said the voice calmly. "Have you nothing to say to me?"

Festini bent his head. For a long time he remained silent.

"I have nothing to say," he said. "You have won and I have lost; that is too obvious to need any labouring."

"Nothing else?" asked the voice.

Festini thought he detected a note of sadness.

"Nothing else," he replied firmly. "What can I say? Except that I lose with a good heart. After all, I have so frequently laid down my creed in regard to such trivial matters as life and death, that even now, confronting the supreme crisis of my life, I can find no more comforting thought than that creed offers."

He heard Tillizini's voice break into a little laugh; a low, amused, yet despairing little laugh.

"How like you, Festini!" he said. "How like you!"

"What else?" asked the Count. "You did not expect me to recant or to offer you terms? You would have despised me as much as I should despise you if you proffered me a way of escape. I suppose," he asked, "you are speaking from some place of security?"

"I am speaking from one of the destroyers," said the other. "We have tapped your wire—"

"Which is cut, I presume," said Festini, coolly.

"Which is cut," repeated the other. "What of Vera?" asked Tillizini suddenly.

"I would rather not discuss that," said Festini, a little haughtily.

"She is with you?"

"Yes, she is here," replied Festini, after a little hesitation. "In justice to myself, I have tried to persuade her to go back. I can conduct her outside these lines without any difficulty."

"And she refuses?"

"Yes, she refuses," said Festini. "And I think it is better so."

He stood with his elbow against the wall, his feet crossed; one who was not acquainted with the circumstances might have thought he was conducting a very ordinary and commonplace conversation, which involved more than ordinary thought, but that had not more than ordinary consequences.

There was another long silence, which Festini broke.

"In all your philosophy, Tillizini," he said, "and I concede you a vast and interesting knowledge of human affairs, has it ever occurred to you how wonderful a thing is a woman? Put out of your mind the passions and the follies of life, and come down to the essentials and the utilitarian part of existence. Is there anything so devoted, so self-effacing, so purely noble? I think," Tillizini heard him laugh, a bright, happy, joyous laugh, "I think that all the bother and stress and scheming of my life, all the crime, as you would call it, all the endeavour and disappointment was worth this: here is my reward, probably more tangible and beautiful than the ten millions we ask from your Government, by the way, I suppose they have adopted you now?" he added, mockingly.

"It is worth much," said Tillizini.

"It is worth all," said Festini, and his voice vibrated; "without this philosophy is futile, life has been wasted."

There was another long pause.

"You have nothing else to say?" asked Tillizini.

"Nothing," said Festini. "Nothing more than I have said. "Is not that enough?" he asked. "What a glutton you are, Tillizini," he bantered him. "What do you desire, a tearful repentance? An admission of my manifold sins and wickednesses? A plea for mercy? King's Evidence?" He laughed again. "You never expected that, my friend?"

"No, I never expected that," said Tillizini's voice. "I don't know exactly what I did expect. I think that is all."

"I will say au revoir," said Festini.

"Farewell," said the other's voice suddenly.

There was such a long wait now that Festini thought the other must have hung up his receiver.

He was on the point of following his example, when Tillizini's voice spoke again.

"And bon voyage!" it said.

Festini laughed, and the receivers clicked together.

The dawn came up greyly over Essex.

Sir Ralph Morte-Mannery, wrapped in furs, dozing in his car, was awakened by the arrival of a pannikin of coffee.

A young officer, great-coated to his ears, held the carriage door open, and smilingly offered it to the other.

"I am afraid it isn't much, Sir Ralph," he said, "but it is all we can give you."

"Is it time?" asked Sir Ralph.

"Nearly," said the other.

Sir Ralph sipped the coffee, and, handing the cup to the waiting orderly, stepped out of the carriage on to the road.

Left and right he saw troops standing under arms, khaki-clad infantry men, line upon line of them. Behind, on a rise, the horses of a field battery were being harnessed to the limbers. In the centre of the river the grim little destroyers lay anchored, a cable's length from one another, and were swinging with the tide.

In the centre of the flat green plain was a house. A long, low-roofed shed was in close proximity. There was no sign of life save for the lazy smoke which rose from the one chimney of the house.

Two mounted officers came cantering up to where the knight stood. One saluted him.

"Good morning, Sir Ralph; your justices are waiting."

He dismounted, and handing the horse to a waiting soldier, the two men walked along the road.

They reached the line of soldiers which were nearest to the house. A long table had been set up in the centre of the road, a table covered with green baize, which was set about by a heterogeneous collection of chairs, commandeered from the neighbouring village.

A man in a tall hat and a fur coat was pacing up and down as Sir Ralph came up. He turned and raised his hat.

"Sir Ralph Morte-Mannery," he said, formally, "I am commissioned by His Majesty's Government to hand you a copy of the Act which was passed last night by the House of Commons and which has received the Assent in the early hours of this morning."

He handed the document to Sir Ralph, who took it with a little bow.

"You will find yourself specified here as the Commissioner to execute the provisions of this Act."

Sir Ralph opened the envelope and took out four closely-printed sheets of paper.

They bore the inscription, "The Preservation of Law Act."

He read the preamble. It was an Act which had been called into existence by the danger which threatened England. He came to that part which defined the Commissioner's duties, and mastered it. Then he stood up by the table, and four men took their places, two on either side.

Sir Ralph removed his hat, and faced the gloomy house.

He read from the document in his hand, and his voice was a little shrill and shaky.

Frank Gallinford, standing a little apart with Tillizini, watched the extraordinary scene with breathless interest. The sense of the tragedy of that moment oppressed him.

He heard the knight's voice quiver as he read the short sentence:—

".... Whereas I, Ralph Morte-Mannery, His Majesty's Commissioner, by this Act appointed, declare all those persons who at present inhabit and sojourn in the place known as Falley's Wharf, in the county of Essex, are persons without benefit of Law, and whereas I declare them to be guilty of a crime, which by this Act is specified as deserving of the punishment of death, now I, by virtue of the power and authority vested in me do pass upon them all, jointly and severally, the sentence which the Law demands, that they shall be shot until they are dead, and their bodies shall afterwards be burnt...."

His voice broke a little. When he had finished reading they saw his lips moving as if in prayer.

Then from the house came the first challenge of the "Red Hand."

There was a distant "click-clock," and Sir Ralph pitched forward over the table, dead.

Festini had seen the ceremony, and guessed its import. He was an excellent marksman....

For twenty-five minutes the fight raged. The Infantry, by short rushes occupying every scrap of cover which the flat plain offered, opened a vigorous fire upon the shed.

Three minutes after the infantry attack had begun the 73rd Battery of the Field Artillery came into action. And simultaneously the destroyers began dropping their tiny shells into the doomed house.

But the "Red Hand" died hard. Shot after shot came from the building. The hut was in flames, part of the house itself was shot away, exposing its bare interior.

Then Frank gripped Tillizini's arm.

"My God!" he said. "Look!"

On the roof-top two figures had suddenly appeared, a man and a woman. The man stood calmly regarding the destructive host that was advancing before him. The woman, Frank saw through his glasses, had her hand upon his shoulder.

Frank reeled back.

"It's Vera!" he gasped.

Tillizini nodded.

"So it seems," he said. "She is a greater woman than I thought."

That was his only comment.

They stood there, a mark for all, but the presence of the woman brought the rifles of the advancing soldiers down. Unscathed they stood. They saw Festini's hand go up in defiance. Then he suddenly tumbled and swayed.

The woman sprang to his side and caught him, holding him close to her breast.

What was plain to be seen by the land force was hidden from the men on the torpedo boats.

Suddenly, right above her head, a shrapnel shell burst, and the two, clasped in one another's arms, sank out of sight as the roof of the burning building collapsed.

Frank turned to Tillizini. The man's face was whiter than usual, and his eyes were wide open, staring.

The Englishman could not speak; he wiped his streaming brow with a handkerchief, and his hand was trembling.

"England owes you something, Professor Tillizini," said Frank, aghast, looking with wonder at the silent figure.

Tillizini made no reply.

When, later in the day, weary and ill-looking, he presented himself at the Premier's house and received the congratulations which the Minister felt were his due, he was more inclined to appraise the part he had played.

"The detection of this gang," said the Premier warmly, "and the destruction of the most dangerous man in Europe, is due entirely to you, Signor Tillizini. You have frustrated him at every turn. It might almost seem," he smiled, "that you were inside his mind and knew what he would do next."

"That is very likely," said Tillizini, absently. "I knew Festini well, and his methods extremely well. I know something of his boyhood, something of his parents, the conditions of his life.

"Old Count Festini had two sons; the elder, for some reason or other, he hated, the younger he petted and spoiled. Count Festini had always been a leader in this type of organization. It is said that he had pursued a vendetta for two hundred years. The old man had put a period to it by destroying the last of the opposition factors.

"It is not the fault of the man who died to-day," he said slowly, "that he was what he was. He was reared and trained to the work, was a ready and willing tool for the 'Red Hand,' until by his very genius he became their master."

"What happened to the elder brother?" asked the Premier curiously.

"I am the elder brother," said Tillizini, and he smiled, a little crookedly.

Richard Horatio Edgar Wallace was born on the 1st April 1875 at 7 Ashburnham Grove, Greenwich. His mother, Mary Jane "Polly" Richards was born into an Irish Catholic family in Liverpool in 1843 and had worked in theatres, both as an actress in bit-parts and as a stagehand and usherette, until she married a Merchant Navy Captain, Joseph Richards, in 1867. He too had been born into an Irish Catholic family in Liverpool. His father had also been a Captain in the Merchant Navy, and his mother's family had a marine background. Mary was eight months pregnant with Joseph's child when he died at sea, and it was once the child had been born that she first turned to the stage, taking the stage name Polly Richards.

She joined the Marriott family theatre troupe in 1872. It was managed by Mrs. Alice Edgar, Richard Edgar, Grace Edgar, Adeline Edgar and Richard Horatio Edgar, Wallace's father. In late 1874 Mary and Richard Horatio Edgar had a brief sexual encounter at the party following a successful show, and she fell pregnant. Worried about the scandal which would ensue and fearing that she might forever lose her job at the troupe, she fabricated an obligation in Greenwich would detain her there for at least six months. She lived in a room in the boarding house on Ashburnham Grove until her son, Edgar, was born. She had already made preparations through her midwife for a couple to foster the child, and when Edgar was born the midwife presented her with Mrs Freeman. Her husband was a fishmonger at Billingsgate market and she already had ten children. She was happy to foster the child and for Polly to make frequent visits to see him in exchange for a small sum of money which Polly made from her work in the theatre troupe.

Wallace was now known as Richard Horatio Edgar Freeman, taking his father's forenames and his foster family's surname. Broadly speaking his childhood was a happy one. The Freemans looked after him lovingly and he had good friendships with his foster siblings, particularly Clara Freeman, twenty years his senior, who often looked after him as a child. After a few years Polly's finances tightened and she was no longer in a position to afford the fee she had been paying the Freemans. However, they had grown to love the young Wallace and opted to adopt him in order to keep him out of the workhouse. Polly could no longer visit him. George Freeman was keen to ensure that he had equal opportunities and did all he could to secure him an education at St. Alfege with St. Peter's, a Peckham boarding school. Despite his adoptive father's efforts, though, Wallace left the school aged twelve for truancy.

Instead he went to work and by the time he was fourteen or fifteen he had experience selling newspapers at Ludgate Circus, near Fleet Street, as a worker in a rubber factory, as a shoe shop assistant, as a milk delivery boy and as a ship's cook. He stole from the milk company which resulted in his dismissal, and in 1894 was engaged to a local girl from Deptford named Edith Anstree, though he broke this off and instead joined the Infantry. He adopted the name Edgar Wallace which he took from Lew Wallace, the author of *Ben-Hur*, and his medical record records a diminutive 33" chest and a stunted growth. his first posting was with the West Kent Regiment in South Africa in 1896, though he did not enjoy military life, arranging to be transferred to the Royal Army Medical Corps. Though this was a less strenuous job, it was also significantly less pleasant and so he again transferred to the Press Corps, which he found suited him far better.

He was in Cape Town in 1898 where he met Rudyard Kipling and was inspired to begin writing and publishing poetry and songs. His first collection of ballads, *The Mission that Failed!* and was enough of a success that in 1899 he paid his way out of the armed forces in order to turn to writing full time. His first work was as a war correspondent for Reuters who kept him in Africa to cover the Boer War, and then for the Daily Mail in 1900 and various other periodicals after that. It was while he was in South Africa that he met and married Ivy Maude Caldecott, who was 21 when they married in 1901, despite her Wesleyan missionary father's strong opposition to the union, for several reasons, one of which was that Wallace's writing was not turning quite the profit he had expected it would. *War and Other Poems* and *Writ in Barracks,* both published in 1900, had not proved as popular as his first collection. Eleanor Clare Hellier Wallace, their first child, died of meningitis in 1903 and, in rather deep debt, they returned to London. Wallace used his contacts with the Daily Mail to get work with them in London, electing to write detective novels as a means of making quick money.

Wallace met Polly, his birth mother, in 1903. He didn't remember her from his childhood as he had been too young when she became unable to visit, so it was as though they were meeting for the first time. She was sixty years old and terminally ill, living in abject poverty. She had come to Wallace seeking financial support, but he turned her away. She died in the Bradford Infirmary later that year. In 1904 he and Ivy had a son, Bryan. He was still writing and had completed his first thriller, *The Four Just Men*. Since nobody would publish it he resorted to setting up his own publishing company which he called Tallis Press and he published a serialised version of *The Four Just Men* in 1905. He received promotional assistance from the Daily Mail in which he ran a competition for entrants to guess the method of murder in the final chapter, with a prize of £1,000 for a correct guess. Although the paper's proprietor, Lord Alfred Harmsworth, refused Wallace the £1,000 prize money, Wallace persisted and went ahead with the competition, recklessly advertising on billboards and buses all over the country, hoping to expand his advertisements across the Empire. His worried colleagues at the Daily Mail managed to convince him to lower the prize money to £500, split into a first prize of £250, a second prize of £200 and a third of £50, but with the total cost of his advertisements nearing £2,000 he would need to sell £2,500 worth of copies before he could see any profit. He was confident that this could be achieved in just three months.

Though he had remarkable enthusiasm, it became clear that his managerial skills left a lot to be desired. It soon emerged that nowhere in the competition terms and conditions had he included a clause limiting the competition to one single winner; instead, any entrant with a winning answer was entitled to their corresponding prize money. Thus, if ten entrants guessed the first prize answer, the competition was obliged to pay each entrant £250. This error was only noticed after the competition had been closed and the solution had been printed in the final installment of the novel, meaning that not only was there no opportunity to write his way out of enormous financial obligation, but the entrants who had guessed correctly would by now have read the final chapter and know they had done so. £250 was an enormous amount of money to the average Edwardian family and those entitled to it were likely to make a lot of noise if they didn't receive their money. Despite this, Wallace's fist instinct was to attempt to ignore the issue entirely, even as he discovered that he initial calculations had been dramatically over-enthusiastic and it would take nearer to two years of continuous sales to break even at the initial cost of £2,500, let alone the new figure which included every correct guesser. Compounding the problem even further was the awful realisation that as sales continued throughout the initial three month period and Wallace approached the £2,500 break-even figure, new readers were still eligible to enter and guess correctly. Though it is unknown how much he eventually owed his readers, Lord Harmsworth found himself having to loan over £5,000 in order to protect the reputation of the newspaper, since 1906 had come around and there still hadn't been a list printed of all prize-winners. It was less a charitable act than one of a man anxious that the failure would reflect ill on his own paper. Wallace filed for bankruptcy shortly thereafter and as a token gesture to his creditors sold the rights to the novel to Sir George Newnes, a publisher and editor, for £75. In the midst of this chaos though, Wallace managed to write and published *Smithy*, which would become the first of a series of *Smithy* novels.

Following this fiascos Wallace was dismissed from the Daily Mail in 1907 when inaccuracies which were found in his reporting, resulting in libel cases being brought against the paper. That year he became the first reporter to be fired from the Daily Mail and was his awful reputation prevented him from finding work at any other papers. Despite all this, though, he travelled to the Congo Free State later that year and reported on the criminal treatment of the Congolese people by King Leopold II of Belgium and the Belgian rubber companies. Up to fifteen million Congolese were killed in various atrocities, and Wallace was asked to serialise stories based on his experiences for her penny magazine *Weekly Tale-Teller*. He and Ivy had another daughter, named Patricia, in 1908. Though his new work for *Weekly Tale-Teller* was bringing in some money, their financial situation was still dire and Ivy was occasionally forced to sell off her jewellery and possessions in order to pay for food. In 1911 his Congolese stories were published in a collection called *Sanders of the River*, which quickly became a bestseller. He would publish eleven more such collections featuring a total of 102 stories of adventure and tribal life set on the river Congo.

From 1908 he started to enjoy a revival of both his success and his reputation. The majority of his initial writing he sold outright in order to make money as quickly as possible and placate his creditors in the United Kingdom and South Africa, but as his success saw the reestablishment of his reputation he began to find work once again as a journalist, beginning in horse racing for the *Week-End*, the *Evening News* and then as an editor for the *Week-End Racing Supplement*. Following this success he started his own racing papers, *Bibury's* and *R. E. Walton's Weekly*, eventually buying his own racehorses and losing thousands gambling. His success was insufficient to support his newly extravagant lifestyle and his marriage began to fail in the light of his financial irresponsibility. He and Ivy had their last child together, Michael Blair Wallace, in 1916, and she filed for divorce in 1918 moving to Tunbridge Wells with her children.

Wallace began to fall for his secretary Ethel Violet King and they married in 1921, having a child, Penelope Wallace, in 1923, who would herself go on to become a successful crime writer. Wallace now began to take his career as a fiction writer more seriously, signing with Hodder and Stoughton in 1921. He now began to organize his contracts more carefully, arranging for royalties and properly organized promotions, run by people more business-minded than himself. He was marketed as the 'King of Thrillers' and they gave him the trademark image of a trilby, a cigarette holder and a yellow Rolls Royce. He was truly prolific, capable not only of producing a 70,000 word novel in three days but of doing three novels in a row in such a manner. His publishers signed off on almost everything he wrote as soon as he turned it in, estimating that by 1928 one in four books being read at any time was written by Wallace, for alongside his famous thrillers he wrote variously in other genres, including but not limited to science fiction, non-fiction accounts of WWI which amounted to ten volumes and screen plays. Eventually he would reach the remarkable total of 170 novels, 18 stage plays and 957 short stories.

Wallace became chairman of the Press Club which to this day holds an annual Edgar Wallace Award, rewarding 'excellence in writing'. In 1923 he broadcasted a report on the Epsom Derby horse race for the British Broadcasting Company, making him the first ever radio sports correspondent. His ex-wife Ivy had suffered from breast cancer between 1923-1924, and it eventually killed her in 1926 despite a successful operation to remove a tumour the year before. He wrote the essay "The Canker in our Midst" in 1926 which dealt, aggressively and controversially, with the problem of paedophilia in show business, describing how children were unwittingly left open to sexual abuse, and linking paedophilia with homosexuality. Its tone has been described as "intolerant, blustering, kick-theblighters-down-the-stairs". He was appointed chairman of the British Lion Film Corporation on the back of the success of *The Ringer* and on the agreement that he give British Lion first choice on all his future work. This contract gave him an annual salary and a large amount of stock with the company, along with a stipend on all British Lion production of his work and 10% of their annual profits. This extraordinary contract gave him annual earnings by 1929 of almost £50,000, or almost £2 million in 2014.

He now became an active figure in politics, entering the 1931 general election as a Liberal contestant in Blackpool, rejecting the current government in favour of free trade. He lost the election by over 33,000 votes and went to America in late 1931, once again deeply in debt after buying the *Sunday News* which closed six months later. In America he quickly found work as a script doctor for RKO Pictures, enjoying early success with the 1932 adaptation of *The Hound of the Baskervilles*. This success, along with that of the play *The Green Pack*, established his reputation in America and he was able to see his own work adapted for film, beginning with *The Four Just Men*. His most successful theatrical work, *On The Spot*, which explores the life of Al Capone, has been described as "arguably, in construction, dialogue, action, plot and resolution, still one of the finest and purest of 20th-century melodramas". These successes led to his assignation on RKO's "gorilla picture" which would become famous as King Kong in 1933.

He worked on the first draft though he was beginning to experience severe headaches which brought about a diagnosis of diabetes. Despite taking medication to address his condition, it deteriorated in a matter of days. His wife booked him passage home but soon heard that he had entered a coma and died of his condition and double pneumonia on the 7th of February 1932 in North Maple Drive, Beverly Hills. In his honour the bell at St. Bride's church on Fleet Street tolled for the duration of the morning while the flags flew at half-mast. He was buried near his home in England at Chalklands, Bourne End, in Buckinghamshire. Once again, at the time of his death he was in severe debt, mostly to racing bookkeepers, though these debts were settled within two years thanks to the enormous royalties his estate continued to receive from his contracts. His writing has been translated into 29 languages, and is considered one of the most important bodies of Colonial writing.

Edgar Wallace – A Concise Bibliography

African Novels
Sanders of the River (1911)
The People of the River (1911)
The River of Stars (1913)
Bosambo of the River (1914)
Bones (1915)
The Keepers of the King's Peace (1917)
Lieutenant Bones (1918)
Bones in London (1921)
Sandi the Kingmaker (1922)
Bones of the River (1923)
Sanders (1926)
Again Sanders (1928)

Four Just Men (Series)
The Four Just Men (1905)
The Council of Justice (1908)

The Just Men of Cordova (1917)
The Law of the Four Just Men (US title: Again the Three Just Men) (1921)
The Three Just Men (1926)
Again the Three Just Men (US title: The Law of the Three Just Men) (1929) a.k.a. Again the Three

Mr. J. G. Reeder (Series)
Room 13 (1924)
The Mind of Mr. J. G. Reeder (US title: The Murder Book of Mr. J. G. Reeder) (1925)
Terror Keep (1927)
Red Aces (1929)[27]
The Guv'nor and Other Short Stories (US title: Mr. Reeder Returns) (1932)

Detective Sgt. (Inspector) Elk series
The Nine Bears or The Other Man or The Cheaters (1910)
revised as Silinski - Master Criminal (1930)
The Fellowship of the Frog (1925)
The Joker or The Colossus (1926)
The Twister (1928)
The India-Rubber Men (1929)
White Face (1930)

Educated Evans (Series)
Educated Evans (1924)
More Educated Evans (1926)
Good Evans (1927)

Smithy (Series)
Smithy (1905)
Smithy Abroad (1909)
Smithy and The Hun (1915)
Nobby or Smithy's Friend Nobby (1916)

Crime Novels
Angel Esquire (1908)
The Fourth Plague or Red Hand (1913)
Grey Timothy or Pallard the Punter (1913)
The Man Who Bought London (1915)
The Melody of Death (1915)
A Debt Discharged (1916)
The Tomb of T'Sin (1916)
The Secret House (1917)
The Clue of the Twisted Candle (1918)
Down under Donovan (1918)
The Man Who Knew (1918)
The Strange Lapses of Larry Loman (1918)
The Green Rust (1919)
Kate Plus Ten (1919)
The Daffodil Mystery or The Daffodil Murder (1920)
Jack O'Judgment (1920)
The Angel of Terror or The Destroying Angel (1922)
The Crimson Circle (1922)

Mr. Justice Maxwell or Take-A-Chance Anderson(1922)
The Valley of Ghosts (1922)
Captains of Souls (1923)
The Clue of the New Pin (1923)
The Green Archer (1923)
The Missing Million (1923)
The Dark Eyes of London or The Croakers (1924)
Double Dan or Diana of Kara-Kara (US Title) (1924)
The Face in the Night or The Diamond Men or The Ragged Princess (1924)
The Sinister Man (1924)
The Three Oak Mystery (1924)
The Blue Hand or Beyond Recall (1925)
The Daughters of the Night (1925)
The Gaunt Stranger or Police Work (1925) revised as The Ringer (1926)
A King by Night (1925)
The Strange Countess (1925)
The Avenger or The Hairy Arm (1926)
'The Black Abbot (1926)
The Day of Uniting (1926)
The Door with Seven Locks (1926)
The Man from Morocco or Souls In Shadows or The Black (US Title) (1926)
The Million Dollar Story (1926)
The Northing Tramp or The Tramp (1926)
Penelope of the Polyantha (1926)
The Square Emerald or The Woman (1926)
The Terrible People or The Gallows' Hand (1926)
We Shall See! or The Gaol-Breakers (US Title) (1926)
The Yellow Snake or The Black Tenth (1926)
Big Foot (1927)
The Feathered Serpent or Inspector Wade or Inspector Wade and the Feathered Serpent (1927)
Flat 2 (1927)
The Forger or The Counterfeiter (1927)
Terror Keep (1927)
The Hand of Power or The Proud Sons of Ragusa (1927)
The Man Who Was Nobody (1927)
Number Six (1927)
The Squeaker or The Sign of the Leopard or The Squealer (US Title) (1927)
The Traitor's Gate (1927)
The Double (1928)
The Flying Squad (1928)
The Gunner or Gunman's Bluff (US Title) (1928)
Four Square Jane or The Fourth Square (1929)
The Golden Hades or Stamped In Gold or The Sinister Yellow Sign (1929)
The Green Ribbon (1929)
The Calendar (1930)
The Clue of the Silver Key or The Silver Key (1930)
The Lady of Ascot (1930)
The Devil Man or Sinister Street or Silver Steel
or The Life and Death of Charles Peace (1931)
The Man at the Carlton or The Mystery of Mary Grier (1931)
The Coat of Arms or The Arranways Mystery (1931)

On the Spot: Violence and Murder in Chicago (1931)
When the Gangs Came to London or Scotland Yard's Yankee Dick
or The Gangsters Come To London (1932)
The Frightened Lady or The Case of the Frightened Lady or Criminal At Large (1933)
The Green Pack (1933)
The Man Who Changed His Name (1935)
The Mouthpiece (1935)
Smoky Cell (1935)
The Table (1936)
Sanctuary Island (1936)

Other Novels
Captain Tatham of Tatham Island or Eve's Island or The Island of Galloping Gold (1909)
The Duke in the Suburbs (1909)
Private Selby (1912)
"1925" - The Story of a Fatal Peace (1915)
Those Folk of Bulboro (1918)
The Book of all Power (1921)
Flying Fifty-five (1922)
The Books of Bart (1923)
Barbara on Her Own (1926)

Poetry Collections
The Mission That Failed (1898)
War and Other Poems (1900)
Writ In Barracks (1900)

Non-Fiction
Unofficial Despatches of the Anglo-Boer War (1901)
Famous Scottish Regiments (1914)
Field Marshal Sir John French (1914)
Heroes All: Gallant Deeds of the War (1914)
The Standard History of the War – Volumes 1 – 4 (1914)
Kitchener's Army and the Territorial Forces:
The Full Story of a Great Achievement (1915)
Vol. 2-4. War of the Nations (1915)
Vol. 5-7. War of the Nations (1916)
Vol. 8-9. War of the Nations (1917)
Famous Men and Battles of the British Empire (1917)
Tam of the Scouts (1918)
The Real Shell-Man: The Story of Chetwynd of Chilwell (1919)
People or Edgar Wallace by Himself(1926)
The Trial of Patrick Herbert Mahon (1928)
My Hollywood Diary (1932)

Screenplays
King Kong (1932, first draft of original screenplay, 110 pages) While the script was not used in its
entirety, much of it was retained for the final screenplay.
The Hound of the Baskervilles (1932, British film)
The Squeaker (1930, British film)
Prince Gabby (1929, British film)

Mark of the Frog (1928, American film)
The Valley of Ghosts (192

Short Story Collections
The Admirable Carfew (1914)
The Adventure of Heine (1917)
Tam O' the Scouts (1918)
The Fighting Scouts (1919)
Chick (1923)
The Black Avons (1925)
The Brigand (1927)
The Mixer (1927)
This England (1927)
The Orator (1928)
The Thief in the Night (1928)
Elegant Edward (1928)
The Lone House Mystery and Other Stories (Collins and son, 1929)
The Governor of Chi-Foo (1929)
Again the Ringer The Ringer Returns (US Title) (1929)
The Big Four or Crooks of Society (1929)
The Black or Blackmailers I Have Foiled (1929)
The Cat-Burglar (1929)
Circumstantial Evidence (1929)
Fighting Snub Reilly (1929)
For Information Received (1929)
Forty-Eight Short Stories (1929)
Planetoid 127 and The Sweizer Pump (1929)
The Ghost of Down Hill & The Queen of Sheba's Belt (1929)
The Iron Grip (1929)
The Lady of Little Hell (1929)
The Little Green Man (1929)
The Prison-Breakers (1929)
The Reporter (1929)
Killer Kay (1930)
Mrs William Jones and Bill (1930)
Forty Eight Short-Stories (George Newnes Limited ca. 1930)
The Stretelli Case and Other Mystery Stories (1930)
The Terror (1930)
The Lady Called Nita (1930)
Sergeant Sir Peter or Sergeant Dunn, C.I.D. (1932)
The Scotland Yard Book of Edgar Wallace (1932)
The Steward (1932)
Nig-Nog and other humorous stories (1934)
The Last Adventure (1934)
The Woman From the East (1934) Co-written By Robert George Curtis
The Edgar Wallace Reader of Mystery and Adventure (1943)
The Undisclosed Client (1963)

Other
King Kong, with Draycott M. Dell, (1933), 28 October 1933 Cinema Weekly

Plays

An African Millionaire (1904)
The Forest of Happy Dreams (1910)
Dolly Cutting Herself (1911)
The Manager's Dream (1914)
M'Lady (1921)
Double Dan (1926)
The Mystery of room 45 (1926)
A Perfect Gentleman (1927)
The Terror (1927)
Traitors Gate (1927)
The Lad (1928)
The Man Who Changed His Name (1928)
The Squeaker (1928)[27]
The Calendar (1929)
Persons Unknown (1929)
The Ringer (1929)
The Mouthpiece (1930)
On the Spot (1930)
Smoky Cell (1930)
The Squeaker (1930)
To Oblige A Lady (1930)
The Case of the Frightened Lady (1931)
The Old Man (1931)
The Green Pack (1932)
The Table (1932)